The Only Way Home

Powder River Publishing

www.powderriverpublishing.com

Also by *Ryan Mitchel Collins*

Everyone Dies Alone 2013

For the Sake of Tomorrow 2016

Table of Contents

Published by:
Powder River Publishing LLC
147 N. Burritt Ave
Buffalo, Wyoming 82834

Copyright © 2021
ISBN: 978-1-7366659-0-9
Printed in the United States of America

The only way home

By Ryan Mitchel Collins

There was never an easy way through any of it for Charlie Porter, especially the truth.

For Charlie, life wasn't about where he'd been, or where he wanted to go. To Charlie, it was about trying to be in the moment. Even when it seemed the past and the future were all-consuming entities geared towards controlling his life for eternity.

'This is what life should be all about, somewhere along the line we got it all wrong," he told himself as he stared out into the tropical night, contemplating the consequences of his life choices. He was desperately awaiting the rising sun when he spotted a white owl flying overhead, his eyes fixed expectantly on the horizon. Charlie had no idea the Hawaiians considered the white owl sacred, he would later come to find that out.

His foes were out there somewhere in the shadows of the Hawaiian bush, amassed, waiting patiently, always pausing for the right moment to rush the lined rental cars awaiting tourists fresh off the plane to drive them.

There were endless vibrantly colored mustangs and plain white Jeeps, all the obvious choices for your typical tourist looking to explore the island in a comfortable, semi stylish and reasonable fashion. The rentals made them stand out, easy for locals to identify so they can treat them accordingly, usually detesting them but always trying to make as much money off them while simultaneously cursing their existence.

When Charlie's foes rushed the parked rental cars at night, they stripped whatever they could in the form of sellable parts before scattering off and stashing what they couldn't carry.

The millionaires who leased the land from the Federal Aviation Administration were too afraid of the messy job of fixing the problem themselves, or of altogether facing a meth problem of that magnitude. In response to these attacks on the rental cars, they deemed it so and sent in a sacrificial lamb to get the job done and that lamb was Charlie Porter.

The millionaires didn't care if there was the possibility of Charlie's death by machete or any small detail of that nature. The only matter of importance here on their end of the deal was to ensure pieces of metal were not sacrilegiously pillaged, or at least not as much. They were willing to pay for someone to be a living presence on the lot.

The very presence of both the meth heads and millionaires was an ominous stench in a sacred landscape, hanging heavy in the air — lurking — always smelled, but not seen until you found the very source itself, which was money and the ability to live in paradise.

Charlie found himself in the height of Trump's America in the last state to join the union, Hawaii. Many claimed he was in the most liberal state in the union, but Charlie had seen his fair share of Trump Republicans and Hawaii Democrats, which he was finding are very conservative.

The people Charlie was tasked with keeping at bay didn't care about all that. They only cared about scouring enough from the cars so they could sell it to someone for pennies on the dollar to get their score. That was all that mattered to them. It was a complex simplicity that brought forth many complications.

They just wanted to get high and forget it all. They wanted to be numb from the pain and endless suffering.

Charlie just wanted to survive and make it through the night in relative comfort with minimal mosquito bites.

It was a tragic cat and mouse affair over rent-a-cars between the millionaires, addicts, and survivalists. Unimaginable wealth in the form of shiny metal rested on the lot with two gates, flanked by unimaginable poverty lurking in the night and a guard named Charlie watching over it all. The only thing he wanted more than some good food was a good night's sleep. After all, he had only been on the island for a few days and hadn't caught a decent night's sleep up to this point.

Charlie's enemies would storm the property when it was

the least guarded throughout the night. That's when they'd spring into action with the ferocity of meth withdrawals, moving seemingly quicker than the rats in the night.

A pack of them stormed the property shortly after the owl had flown overhead. Charlie watched their beleaguered movement with rising panic searing through his chest.

They were a brazen bunch, not caring if the glare of his headlights beamed into their eyeballs. No deterrence in the least. It encouraged them to move faster as they headed toward his van with malevolence. Charlie fumbled rolling down the window then started taking pictures with shaking hands, not knowing what would happen if they reached his van.

"They're gonna shred my ass to pieces," he thought to himself. "I'll have to kill a few of them with my bare hands to get away. It's not going to be easy or pretty, but I'll have to do it."

They scattered like a pack of cockroaches after seeing the camera, jumping into their cars that were hidden out of sight in the bushes, peeling down the road into the blooming February morning.

"The camera scared them off," he said to himself in disbelief.

Charlie called in the encounter with airport security like he was instructed to do. Airport security arrived 20 minutes later and scolded Charlie for calling them away from their morning coffee. It was the way the island worked for him so far.

"Trespassing is not a crime," the security guard said, before shaming him for drinking a beer at 6 a.m. "If you want to be a real security guard, you need to act like it."

Charlie acted as if he was taking his advice to heart, but in reality was just another failed mainlander who just got to the island, living out of the back of a van temporarily in exchange for "light security" duty and "work trade."

It was the dawning of his 6th day on the island of Kauai. He, just like many others, was desperately seeking housing that was nonexistent there, but constantly demanded. Like a prehistoric caveman, Charlie was seeking that all-important dwelling to place the valuables that had no value to anyone but himself.

"Even those meth heads have tent cities," he said to himself. "What the hell is wrong with me?"

There was a degree of difficulty here that he hadn't experienced in any other of his tramping across the states and the world. He was starting to crack up at the seams due to all the craziness surrounding his short time there, not even a full week into it now.

The middle-aged security guard called in the real police to check and see if Charlie had any warrants. The security guard also wanted to teach Charlie a lesson and see if his story checked out.

"I'm just going to call them in and make sure everything is good, brudda," he said to Charlie.

The two waited in silence as Charlie finished his beer and lit a cigarette to hide the smell of beer on his breath. The security guard just shook his head as he responded to a call on the radio asking where he was because they couldn't find him.

"Like I said before, you take a left at the second gate," he explained into the radio. "You're at the first one. It's the one that's padlocked. The next one is the one."

When they arrived, two muscle-bound men got out of their cars, surrounding Charlie. He nervously tried to explain his task of watching the lot at night to keep the cars from getting broken into.

"Who owns this land?" they asked him forcefully.

"The Federal Aviation Administration," Charlie responded after thinking about it for a minute.

They didn't believe him in the slightest despite it actually being Federal Aviation Administration land.

It was only when he informed them he was the only government reporter on island that they took him seriously, leaving quicker than they had got there in the first place, which was not very fast.

When they left, he drove the busted up van that had got totaled and parked on the lot without a license plate or back window, down to Hanamaulu Bay, a few hundred yards from the lot. It was whale season after all and Charlie had never seen a whale.

He got there in time to watch the sun slowly meander over

the ocean and into the morning sky, setting the sleepy Pacific horizon aflame.

No whales were to be seen, but there were busses of tourists arriving with whale seeking enthusiasts coming from all directions and corners of the world. They unloaded in flocks, wearing thick layers of suntan lotion and white tennis shoes, sporting enthusiastic but serious looks on their faces.

"It will be different here," he thought to himself, knowing better deep down.

"There were missions upon missions here that could not be pulled off by anyone of normal mind and spirit. Only by the one with the true Aloha spirit can make it," he told himself. "Mucho Aloha, but with the trepidation of one's mortality."

The Island could eat a man like Charlie up and swallow him whole in a matter of minutes. It happened every day. His friends and family were semi worried about him and had been for some time now, but he cared not for their concerns and always pushed on without conceding to others.

Charlie wasn't the only one the island could eat up in minutes and he tried to keep that in mind.

There had been a murder-suicide on Valentine's Day, a few days before. The newspaper Charlie worked for received a press release from the county as to what they had found from their "investigation" into the matter. The deceased man washed up on the shore roughly a mile apart from his wife. They were both dead and the man was missing his feet. The wife had signs she had been "assaulted" as the county put it in their first press release, as in blunt trauma wounds.

Charlie's colleague Daniel was on the story from the get-go.

Daniel was a tall drink of water, originally from Texas before moving to the East Coast to work for a few newspapers in the Maryland area. He stood a skinny 6' 6" but had the demeanor of a teenager waiting to get drunk at his first party, mixed with the cunning of a military intelligence officer—which is what he did during his time in service.

The county of Kauai controlled the narrative on all information released to the public and media like Charlie and Daniel. It was state-run media in its hypothetical existence, much-touted of late by the Trump administration and alive in Hawaii.

Late at night, Jason and Charlie would drunkenly scheme about how to destroy this monster created far before either of their arrivals on the island.

"Would anyone believe a story like this about what is really happening here?" Charlie would say to Daniel. "It's almost too crazy to be true. There are roving groups of Hawaiian ice fiends running around, making the junk in a village near where the cars are parked. The guards know all of their names and went to high school with them. The tweakers occasionally get arrested on this or that charge, but are always released because they 'stink up the jail.' It's an endless parade of stealing this or stabbing that person, and then they're out of jail within a week. And if they aren't let out of jail, they have free rent and three meals a day. They have a good system worked out and the system loves them. I wonder how many tourists they kill each year?"

Daniel, the cops and court reporter never looked into it. Daniel knew better and valued his time on the island too much to go messing around breaking up rackets of any sort without proper approval.

"This entire thing is built for them, around them, but not to help them in the least. There's no profit in helping them. They would rather spend ten times the amount playing a cat and mouse game. It's sport for the bored millionaire," Charlie told Daniel one night.

"You're missing the point," Daniel said in response, opening another beer under the vast Hawaiian stars. "You're the fucking sacrificial lamb here. These goddamn millionaires will eat you for breakfast while fighting the crackheads tooth and nail, only to lose in a landslide, and fuck you over in the process."

Daniel's words of a conflicting nature to the desperation always sank into Charlie's head.

"There's no entertaining reason and logic on this goddamn island." he would say in response.

Trying to watch Humpback whales breach the morning he was rushed by the meth heads was the kind of thing that mattered to Charlie and all that other bullshit would have to take a backseat and wash away, but it was a thing he knew he would have to face eventually.

They cooked the meth and were living off the land near the bay. This he knew, or at least he surmised from what he was told after looking into it.

This situation was an absolute nightmare for the powers that be, he thought to himself.

"To have tweakers that are self-dependent and living off the land creates a unique wave in the undercurrents of society. There had to be some involvement by the local police department. It's the only way to make sense of the entire situation. How else could you explain how the cops refused to do anything about the rash of car parts stolen of late? There was an element of them making money off this situation and I can smell it all the way from the mainland," he said to himself looking for whales. He was practicing a way to pitch the story to his editor, who was from Idaho. Later he talked to his editor about the situation, trying to say it the way he practiced to himself.

His editor was blown away and most of all mistrusting, but like most of the middle-aged men in his position, he was painfully out of touch with the matters that mattered. He didn't have the basic constitution needed to deal with things of this nature. Nor did he care.

Charlie failed to understand this with his rational approach to the irrational.

The entire cat and mouse concept made the editor hesitate. There wasn't enough human interest to the piece, he thought to himself. He wouldn't mess with it until someone got killed he figured. He was in charge, the editor-in-chief. He'd been on island for seven years now.

Nobody was going to tell him a damn thing, especially some kid from god knows where who was living in a van fending off these monsters.

Ever so often early in the day, the editor would call Charlie into his office and close the door to tell him how unbelievably crazy and mixed-up the island was. How he wasn't sure if he could afford to live here. That it was all just so backward and mucked up there was no fixing it ever or even trying to do so for that matter. He believed firmly the future of the island was more congestion and constipation.

There was no changing this rock in his mind and Charlie respected his tenured opinion, but his editor had tendencies that alarmed him. The editor had a habit of talking to himself. Not just the common mumble to oneself every now and again, but full-blown conversations with himself.

There was no blaming him for the conversations Charlie thought. It was the only way to deal with all of the insanity that made absolutely no sense at the end of the day and one had to deal with it in some manner. That was the way his editor had chosen to deal with it. It made sense to Charlie looking at it that way.

After all, Charlie was busy working on an article about a missing kid from Maine named Alexander and couldn't be bothered by rackets and talking to oneself. Alexander, like Charlie, had come to the island seeking god knows what and had got himself missing for a year. His trail had gone cold and his bank account had not been used since February 22, 2018, exactly a year ago to the day Charlie was watching for whales in the bay.

The article about Alexander was set to run the next morning. It was the start of something, but of what Charlie hadn't a clue. He never saw a whale on the island that morning, or ever for that matter. Only monk seals, sea turtles and lots of white owls graced his presence.

The way here

It was one of the hardest goodbyes of Charlie Porter's life. He began to get emotional.

"I don't know, it's nearly impossible to say goodbye to her now. How long did I know her? A few months," Charlie wondered to himself. "They're all hard goodbyes. She should just get on the plane and come with me and quit all this pretending. That's what someone who really cares would do, I think."

He was parked, sitting in the cab of a small red truck in the parking lot at the Moab, Utah airport crying like a teenager in love. He was leaving to Hawaii after running a small newspaper in San Juan County for four months.

Charlie fell in love again, he'd had fallen in love with the land and a woman of the land in Utah now, but now it was time to leave, again. She was steeped in the land and the culture of those canyonlands. She would show him all she knew of it. It was in her genes as she told him over the months they spent together exploring and laughing, both wounded souls trying to find something to help live again.

"Don't get on that plane," Mary told Charlie, crying and lost in his arms, knowing deep down they would never see each other again. "Stay here with me, Porter."

He knew he had to get on that plane, there was no other way about it in this universe. It was something that had to be and he didn't know why. All he knew was he must go and not look back. If she were to come, then things might be different, but he had to go. Of this he was certain.

They were opposites in every sense of the word. She was an activist for the "cause" and he was an editor who was branded a supporter of the very thing she was fighting against — the designation of a National Monument at Bears Ears.

Before they met, Charlie's time in the Canyonlands was spent writing and drinking. It was a rinse and repeat type cycle that seemed to help him pass the time away. Everything had lost meaning — life had lost its luster in his eyes after losing his son to Wyoming and his mother's scorn.

It felt necessary for Charlie to souse himself nightly in a numb wash to process the pain and the loss of his young family. He was searching for something there within the land.

The vibrantly striking Slickrock that captivated the eyes and minds of Edward Abbey and Everett Ruess also caught the soul and mind of Charlie Porter.

Charlie would throw himself at the land and get lost within it. Consumed by its vastness and grandeur, finding peace in the silence and echoes within emptiness.

Charlie slowly started to get better.

One night he wrote a letter to his son until he fell asleep, trying to make sense of his life as the wind rocked his humble establishment in the desert dark, almost to the point of tipping over at times.

"I came to San Juan County in early October of 2018. It was raining when I arrived and it didn't stop for a week. It was the most rain they have had here in decades. The town of Monticello was in a dangerous drought, to the point of having to conserve culinary water. The consensus is if there's not a serious snowpack this winter, then they will be in serious trouble this summer. The previous summer, the town had been forced to conserve water due to the drought and they weren't allowed to water their yards and it upset lots of the locals of course.

Despite the constant droughts that are a part of life in the desert, people keep moving here in droves even if there isn't close to enough water to support them all. The infrastructure can't sustain the sheer numbers of people demanding a certain way of life in the frontier. They want this certain kind of life without having to give up conveniences they were used to in the old life. It doesn't dawn on them they were never meant to live here, including me. It's the land of the Navajo now. Before them, it was the land of the Anasazi or ancient ones who built their dwelling in the cliffs.

Monticello stood out to me. The Mormon settlers who founded the town named it after Thomas Jefferson's estate, fol-

lowing lots of arguments about what to name it. They decided
Monticello was a better fit than Hammond, Antioch, or North
Montezuma Creek. Hammond was the name of their Mormon
leader and the younger generation of settlers wasn't very keen on
raising their family in the name of Hammond. They decided on
Monticello.

The Blue Mountains hang pristine above the sleepy little
town of 2,000 that saw its boom during the 1950s, supported by
the bountiful uranium mines that provided the engine for progress. The biggest thing to happen to the area in the previous 50
years was the designation of Canyonlands as a national park and
the designation of Bears Ears as a national monument.

I noticed immediately the local residents have a sticker on
their vehicles with a bear on it that reads "no monument."

Before I picked up and moved here, there was a nasty fight
to pull the designation of Bears Ears as a national monument by
President Obama on December 28, 2016. He designated the 1.2
million acres a national monument in the final days of his presidency after creating a tribal coalition of local native political
leaders. They listened to the tribal coalition, most likely out of an
ability to gain something, and out of the coalition came the new
monument.

Donald Trump came next. One of the first things he and his
pal Orrin Hatch did was to re-designate the newly created national
monument into two segmented sections that didn't even include
the two hills that are the literal Bears Ears. The two-segmented
factions of the redesignated monument were the Indian Creek
unit, which borders Canyonlands National Park, and the Shash
Jáa unit to the south. The redesignated monument now stands at
201,876 acres after Trump rescinded it on December 4, 2017. It
was a reduction of nearly one million acres.

I am coming in after the great raking over the coals for the
past year, and now, the issues are beginning to explode at the
seams. This will be my job as the managing editor of the San Juan
Record, to tell the tale. A publication that has been churning the
presses since 1915, telling strange stories only the desert can produce. Only those strange stories and things that can be conjured

up by a journey through life while in the desert.

Moab is a spectacle now. A nonstop tourist train aimed at hitting the heart of it all as quickly as possible while spending the least, but in turn spending an ungodly amount of coin while merely experiencing the peripherals of what the desert has to offer for the wayward soul. There is nothing within yourself that can't be cured by the desert I have been told.

The first days are always spent getting your bearings about you here. It takes a little bit of adjustment. You're no good to anyone if you can't figure out where you are exactly in the world at a given time. I've seen too many poor souls, wandering about, headed to the Navajo Reservation in the middle of the night, hitchhiking their way to expel whatever is ailing them. They, just like all of us, are trying to find their way through all the extremities that stick to us and destroy us, but make us inevitably stronger through the process, or simply just kill us.

The rain has continued in hard and unending succession for weeks now. I had my introduction to what the experience would be like for me here. It's different for everyone, wherever you go. It depends on who you are and what you are there for.

There is no housing in this Southeastern Utah now. I was tasked with finding a place before I got there in an area where there is zero housing available and the hotels run in the area of $1,000 a week. I looked in the classified ads of the paper I was going to be tasked with managing and I found an advertisement that had been running consecutively for as long back as I could see for a, "one and two-bedroom trailers in good condition."

So I arranged for one of these said trailers, the only one available that was not ready to move into yet. The owner told me that I would have to live amongst all the grand construction planned for the place before winter hit. He agreed to drop the rent and told me that I would just have to be patient while they got the place up and running.

"No problem," I said. "Just as long as I have a roof over my head."

This didn't sound like that bad of a deal considering there was no other possible place to keep my plants and your cat while

I waited the storm out. There was a necessity to have something the second I got here, so the decision was an easy one, and I decided to put my laurels aside and take what I could get. After all, the people I worked with, I thought, would lead me to something better when they saw what means I would have to go through to be here and do the job that was needed.

When I got here, I towed my 1999 Honda Civic, which I drove across the country from Canada to Mexico, with a used 2001 Chevy S10 I had just bought for the move. I made the five-hour drive from Vernal to Monticello, from one beehive to the other, a week before. I had made the drive down to Monticello a few weeks earlier to meet with the publisher and look the area over to be sure I could hang my hat there for at least six months before they fired me. It didn't seem like a bad place, but they all told me finding a house there would be nearly impossible. So when I got the job and the place and was nearly there, I felt as if there was nothing that couldn't be done with sheer will and determination. When I pulled up to the place with your cat under my seat stuck, and my plants wilting from the stress of the move, I was tired and starving and desperately needed to find sanctuary.

The landlord lived next door and sauntered out of his modular home, which was the castle of the trailer park that was a tornado's dream. The older obese gentleman was nice enough and gave me a longer than wanted tour of the house that was falling to pieces after winters and brutal summers in the high desert town. Your cat was set free from the confines of the car and the plants were loaded into the house and I made my bed before I passed out due to exhaustion.

The entrance was sudden, the patience thin. I was coming into the battle. It wasn't that significant to me to begin with, it was just another thing in a long chain of journeys that usually lead to the same thing in the end, which is looking for another place to go. It's a pattern that's easy to get into when the world is in the place it is.

I went to Mesa Verde on my third day calling Monticello home, trying to escape the rain which had settled over the Colorado Plateau. I crossed into the familiar territory of my home state of Colorado, but the area I was exploring there was also new to me. Cortez was the nearest town of any significance as far as shopping and materials needed to function in the desert.

Only the essential things that Walmart could provide for the adventurer on a budget, looking to explore the ancient breadbasket of the Puebloans with the proper gear to get it done without getting too uncomfortable while doing it.

Cortez also had the most retail marijuana stores I have ever seen in my life. I counted 15 while driving through town. The biggest of which looked over the town with a magnificent white flag and a green cross waiving in the wind on top of the highest mesa near the center of town.

Sleeping Ute Mountain greets you as you come into town from Monticello, always eager to get out of Utah, not necessarily because of the land, but because of the way people stare at you when you're buying 3.2 percent alcohol at the gas station or grocery store because you prefer to steer away from the "state liquor store" that is open only until 6 p.m. The closeness to Colorado was the only reason I accepted the job and knew that I could handle it. Being 13 miles from the Colorado border while living in Utah was the only way I could be in the state. If you get too deep into Utah, it's dangerous for one's soul. You can meander into the heart of it if you have important business to do or to catch a flight, but Salt Lake City is something to avoid at all costs. Even the air there is poisonous not to mention the politics.

I went to Durango and checked out the town I had always heard about, but had never been to. The old mining town quickly faded into my rear mirror as fast as it had come and I was on the way to the Indian Casino at Ignacio, just near the New Mexico border.

I had no idea what to expect and I was pleasantly surprised when I pulled up to the casino on the Saturday night, the place brimming with activity. The parking lot was packed full and the air seemed contagious in the fall evening where the possibility of losing all the money I had until my first payday was a real threat. So I played very lightly at first, feeling out the casino and observing the ins and outs of this foreign money machine that seemed to house the entire Navajo Nation, who were having beers and quietly pulling away at the reels of destiny.

The line to the buffet was overflowing and I went and had a much-needed dinner that set my spirit straight and prepared me for the battle that lay ahead. I went to the poker table and battled it out for five hours until I could not play another minute. I walked out with $100 more than I came in with and decided I would try and get some sleep in the parking lot of the casino.

It didn't work as I tossed and turned in the uncomfortable vehicle before I turned the key to drive down the dark October road for an hour and a half before making the turn into my house. I wonder what I would be doing if you were here with me Joyce? I have a feeling I wouldn't be doing any of it.

All of these things I am doing are because I cannot be with you now son. If I were with you and things were different, none of this would have ever happened and we may all have been the better for it. But this is where I am now and this is how I will have to make my way home to you, through all of these trials and trails until the road leads home to you again."

Charlie fell asleep after writing a letter to his son he hoped he would read someday in the distant future when he would be able to understand just what it is that his father had gone through. He knew his son would never read the letter, but it felt good to him to believe that it made things better somehow.

San Juan County

The first article Charlie wrote for the San Juan Record was an opinion editorial entitled, "Being a good Samaritan is something that never goes out of style, regardless if you're a millennial." The central theme of the introductory piece was to explain the fortuitous meeting Charlie had with longtime San Juan County Commissioner Adam Bruce, a Mormon Bishop and local Republican stalwart.

It ran on October 23, 2018:

*** * * * * * * * ***

This article will be a little dated by the time it hits the newsstands, but like someone once told me, a good story shouldn't have a shelf life.

This isn't a classic or anything like that, but it was a story I don't think I'll forget anytime soon.

It was just one of those things in life like many others that has a tendency to compound over the course of a day when things are going a certain way. They were certainly going a certain way that Saturday.

This story I must warn our readers will be a little damning for the author, but humility never hurt anyone as far as I'm aware. It all started early that morning, fresh off a snow in the mountains. I headed north to Grand County and that eternally busy Moab, where everything seems to be coming and going at all times, no matter the month or season.

I was destined to spend some time with Jenny Wilson, whom some of our readers may have read about last week.

Some may have skipped over that story after reading the first few words if they got that far. This has a little to do with that meeting with Wilson.

This story really starts when I said goodbye to Mrs. Wilson and headed in the opposite direction. They asked me to come to lunch with them after spending the better part of the morning together, but I politely declined, saying, "I must be on my way back to San Juan County." I thanked them for their time and headed South.

I know it's 50 miles, I've driven it at least 20 times now over the course of the past month. I know that it consumes more gas than you think, but in one of those brilliant flashes of pure stubbornness that never turns out very well – other than to learn lessons – I carried on without filling my tank.

I've cut it close before in this car, and I have always counted on the tested fact that when it hits the yellow gaslight, I have around 40 miles to get to a pump before I'm walking to the gas station.

So when the yellow light came on and I was 20 miles outside of Monticello, I calmly thought to myself that I had this one in the bag and it really shouldn't be a problem for me to make it into town.

But as I started to climb Peters Hill, I felt the engine do the first momentary give out, signaling the gas light wasn't messing around. I would try and ease the manual into a different gear to get some catch, but before long I saw the writing on the wall.

I calmly continued to try to gain ground to the top of the hill before beginning the long walk into town. It was a nice enough afternoon and there was no trouble in walking. It would actually be a good opportunity to see the six miles leading into Monticello from the North.

I grabbed the gas can from my trunk and started the walk into town. A quick look behind me after fifteen or so minutes gave me an idea of the progress I had made, and it wasn't much. Maybe just over a mile from the looks of it.

I knew that I was about six miles outside of town, judging by the odometer which I had reset just when I was leaving Moab that read 44 miles.

Rudimentary math danced around in my head (it was never

my strong suit in school) about distance and time. Glancing at my phone, I figured this would take up a big portion of my afternoon.

I would get into town and either get a ride or drive my truck to the beached car and fill it enough to get back to town and get a ride at some point.

It may have been my matching red gas can, but before long a red truck pulled over, and when I approached the cab, I saw there was no room in the front, so I signaled to the driver and passenger that I was going to jump in the back.

They gave the thumbs up, and I jumped in the bed of the truck as the driver sailed down the road the moment I sat down. The wind sped through my hair, almost blowing off my sunglasses as the driver picked up speed into the October afternoon.

I got a look at the countryside with the stark cold of the early winter hitting the edges of my eyes and mouth, making me keenly aware of the oncoming winter season as I glanced at the glistened Abajos.

"These guys are pretty nice," I thought to myself in the back of the truck, kicking myself for not filling up in Moab, thus avoiding the entire situation.

When we came to town, the red truck went past the first gas station and went to the second in town.

When I got out of the back, the driver of the red truck informed me that he was going to go grab an air tank and he would be back in a few minutes to fill it up at the air station, pointing to the filling station a few hundred feet away.

The man said he would give me a ride back to my car because he had to go out to his ranch and do some work after he filled the tank. I looked at the two men, one significantly older than the other, and I was a baby compared to the two of them. I heartily thanked the two, telling them that I truly appreciated the gesture.

I got my gas and ten minutes went by before I started to get a little nervous that I may have messed the meeting place up as the driver pointed to "over there."

I began to look around Blue Mountain Foods and the surrounding buildings before the red truck pulled up next to me and the driver, half laughing, said, "I'm going to fill my compressor up at that tank over there." He pointed to the big air tank just behind me.

I laughed with them and walked over to the tank, as they got out of the truck and began to fill the small compressor in the bed of the truck.

The driver stuck his hand out at me and introduced himself as Commissioner Adam Bruce. I took a double-take at him and told him that I had seen him on television before and that I was the new editor in town.

It was Adam's father with him I was later told, and they both looked at each other and gave a big grin. We had fun with the circumstance for a second before they were done filling the compressor up.

"I feel really bad there isn't room up in the cab," Adam said to me.

"Beggars can't be choosers," I told him as I gladly hopped in the back of the truck and we were down the road again.

We got to the beached vehicle, and Adam got out of the truck and came and helped me get the car running again. He wanted to make sure I got it running before he left. It turned over on the second try.

"You're sailing again," he told me as I thanked him and informed him I owed him one. "We take care of each other around here," he said to me.

What an interesting way to meet the chair of the County Commission. I want to say thank you again to Adam and his father for taking the time out of their busy life and helping a stranger in need. It was a good thing to do, especially when they discovered I was the new editor.

In the end, I thanked him as a "gentleman and a scholar" and learned that being a good Samaritan truly never goes out of style, even if you're a millennial like myself.

****

After the first county commissioner meeting Charlie covered for the paper, not long after Bruce had given him a ride that day, he came into Charlie's office and asked for a copy of the paper he could give to his wife.

Charlie happily fulfilled Bruce's request knowing sooner than later there would be a battle between the two of them in some form and it would be good to start it off nice. It was the eventuality of the subject. Charlie being a native Coloradoan and Bruce being the Utah Mormon rancher, who was related to the founder of the town of Monticello and his great-great-grandfather was buried down the road in the village of Bluff, Utah, which was founded in 1880.

Charlie's claim to fame was an Uncle who sold weed legally in Colorado, and that he was related to William Henry Harrison, who was his, "second great-great-great-uncle, or something like that."

When Charlie was young, he was told Harrison refused to wear a coat during his inauguration. Harrison died on April 4th 1841.

"A true stubborn asshole to the last. My kin." Charlie often said of Harrison.

Adam Bruce, however, was a giant player in the Republican party in San Juan county. When Donald Trump shrunk Bears Ears National Monument in 2017 with a stroke of his pen in Salt Lake City, Bruce was there wearing a cowboy hat that read, "Make San Juan County great again." He and Phil Lynman were grand old friends and served on the county commission together. Their ancestors were part founders of both Blanding and Monticello, true believers of the Latter Day Saints from the word go.

Bruce carried with him the guaranteed prospect of winning the election again for the third time in District 1, which was just around the corner. He was running uncontested for the seat and was the Republicans only chance of maintaining the semblance of power he and others like him had had in that area since they colonized it in the 1880s.

Bruce would have made a fine governor many in the community thought, including himself.

What made the whole ordeal essential to Charlie as a ragtag

journalist and wannabe writer was the backdrop of Bears Ears and the fact a federal judge had recently redistricted the county earlier that year to combat gerrymandering. The judge made the order to give the Native Americans, especially those that lived on the Navajo Nation reservation, the right to have their population, which was the majority population in the county, fair representation in their respective local government.

The same people that lauded president Trump when he rescinded the monument Obama had established there, hated the redistricting with all of their hearts and money. Adam Bruce and his fellow commissioners Jessa Anally and Phil Lynman, nearly bankrupt the county's general fund fighting the redistricting. It came out later they even paid a hefty lawyer bill twice by mistake.

The three commissioners were in their final month together when Charlie arrived in San Juan County to take over newspaper operations for the San Juan Recorder, a month before the historic election was to take place.

Lynman was the man who rode with the infamous Oregon BLM standoff Bundy boys at recapture canyon on their ATVs beyond the BLM's ATV boundary in 2014. Recapture Canyon was closed down to motorized vehicles by the BLM in 2007 to protect the Anasazi cliff dwellings and cultural artifacts that are extremely prevalent there. Lynman and hundreds of supporters rode their ATVs across the Rubicon that was the BLM boundary and he was promptly arrested. Considered a martyr in their symbolic fight against the federal government, Lynman fought the charges in court and spent a lot of money doing so, most of which was donated by the community Charlie was told. They despised the idea of the federal government and wanted the national parks under local control.

Ultimately Lynman was found guilty of trespass and conspiracy, both of which were misdemeanors and he was sentenced to 10 days in jail. They slapped him with a $96,000 fine, of which he elected to pay off in installments of $100 with a co-defendant who was also charged with Lynman because he promoted it on his website before the protest. Later, Lynman sued the BLM for punitive damages for an amount not less than $10 million. The matter was later dropped when Lynman failed to notify the Federal Government of his lawsuit and it was dropped.

Little did Charlie know, but Lynman would be pardoned by president Trump in his last days of office in 2021. Trump called Lynman a, "man of integrity and character," who was, "subjected to selective prosecution" by the Obama administration.

When Lynman was sentenced in 2016 to 10 days in jail, he had the opportunity to make a dramatic speech about the evils of the federal government. Instead, he cried about having to go to jail for 10 days. Now, Charlie had come at a time when redemption was in the air for Lynman who was headed to the Utah House of Representatives to now make the laws and exact vengeance on the men who put him in jail, the federal government and judges. His bosses to some extent now, who he pledged to hold accountable.

"Going into this, you know, I've said a number of times, I'm a foot soldier," Lynman told National Public Radio in 2017. "I'm not a captain. I'm not a general. I'm willing to die on a battlefield for a good cause."

Lynman was sentenced by Federal District Judge David Nuffer, who was appointed by Barack Obama in 2011 and decided to redistrict San Juan County in 2017 into three different districts as represented by population. Lynman appealed the ruling and sentencing in his Recapture Canyon protest ride case, citing bias by Nuffer against him. The sentence was upheld and Lynman served his time and won reelection to the San Juan County commission. Then went on to win consecutive terms in the Utah House of Represenatives.

Lynman, cognizant of the fact he would not defeat Willie Grayeyes in the county commissioner race of November 2018 due to the redistricting and now all-powerful Navajo vote, ran for the Utah house of representatives with greater political apsiration in mind. The former commissioner and CPA was posed to win by a landslide over his opponent Lisha Hall, who was a granola type and believed the economy in Utah should be focused on the tourism.

Lynman believed it should be run with pure oil and coal, and of course opportunistic development and ranching.

At Charlie's first county commission meeting, he was weighed by the powers that were on their way out as a new enemy. They had been grilled by the Salt Lake Tribune for years now, especially Lynman, over their ideology and spending. The commissioners had concealed their spending nicely up to that point and Charlie was semi accepted because of the ride Adam Bruce had given him. Charlie sat through the first meeting, like he always did in long meetings of this type. And as usual, he was in disbelief at the way the local government operated there in broad daylight.

On his way out the door Adam Bruce asked him, "Is there anything else, Charlie?"

He seized the opportunity and approached Lynman who was seated next to Bruce and told him he'd interviewed his opponent in the upcoming House of Representatives race recently for an article, where Hall had told Charlie that she was legitimately scared of Lynman. Charlie added she would not do the interview if he asked her about Proposition 2, which was a ballot initiative placed by the voters to vote on medical marijuana.

"I would love to talk to you about Proposition 2," he said. "I have no problem talking about controversial things."

They went into a little room with a rocking chair Charlie sat in and rocked back and forth as he stared into Lynman's eyes and asked him about the economy, medical marijuana and the future of San Juan County and Utah in general.

Lynman was one of the good old boys. His family was one of the most prominent families there. They had made moves for generations in order to get one of theirs in a position of power like Lynman was.

He was a soft-spoken man, hardly the kind of guy in Charlie's opinion that was to be felt afraid of. But Charlie had lived in the Dominican Republic and had shotguns pulled on him before, so he was scared of different things than most.

Charlie was pretty sure Hall was scared of him too. She caught onto the fact he was hungover during their interview and asked him if he was alright. Charlie confessed he was going through a nasty custody battle and how much it weighed on him day and night.

She told him that she was sorry to hear that and wished him luck with, "a good resolution at some point."

When Charlie asked Lynman why Hall would say something like she was afraid of him, he said, "she is just being funny."

In the next weekly edition of the paper, which ran on Wednesdays and only once a week on account of the low circulation, Charlie ran the one on one interviews with each of the respective candidates of the San Juan County Commissioner race and the local Utah House of Representatives race. The commissioner race was lining up to be historic for the prospect of having the first Navajo County Commission majority since "800 A.D." as his boss put it.

Lynman won the Utah House by a landslide, along with the Navajo activist County Commissioner Willie Grayeyes in District 2, Republican Bruce in Commissioner District 1, and Navajo activist Kenny Maryboy in District 3.

On November 7th, Charlie wrote his account of that election night and the historic results that followed under the headline, 'Historic election provides a monumental shift from past for San Juan County.'

It read—

"San Juan County Clerk/Auditor Juan Nielson calls in from Monument Valley to the polling station in Monticello at the courthouse. His cell phone service cuts in and out, as he attempts to give information about the Monument Valley count. His phone drops the call.

It's 9:10 p.m. on Election Day, one hour after the polls closed.

Deputy County Clerk James Francom calls in right after Nielson with information from Montezuma Creek. He's just outside of Blanding, headed back to Monticello with a lockbox of counted ballots, as poll workers and county staff battle yawns and fatigue.

India Nielsen, a Special Assistant with the Lieutenant Governor's office, tails Francom on the way to the clerk's office. She's been tasked with observing the polling station Francom manned throughout the day.

Nielsen is unfamiliar with the area and follows Francom to Monticello, not to observe the transport of the ballots, but rather to avoid getting lost on the 60 mile drive through the dark desert terrain.

Nielsen and the Lieutenant Governor's office aren't the only ones monitoring the polling station that day. The Department of Justice and the Rural Utah Project also have officials looking over operations.

The subject of discussion back in the clerk's office in Monticello centers around when official results will be available. If they count all the estimated 800 mail-in ballots grouped together in boxes and lockboxes on the floor, in addition to official results for Monument Valley, Montezuma Creek, and Navajo Mountain, the evening could run into the morning.

Francom emerges through the doors of the San Juan County Courthouse with the lockbox full of counted ballots from Montezuma Creek. The group waits for county clerk Nielson as he drives through the night headed for Monticello.

Nielson arrives with the ballots from Monument Valley more than an hour after Francom.

The only remaining ballot box is being driven by Delton Pugh from Navajo Mountain. Pugh volunteered for the four and a half-hour drive the day before. There is virtually no cell service on the trip. He did it because the person who had previously volunteered canceled at the last minute.

Salt Lake City media waits in the lobby, as they hope for the results of the San Juan County Commissioner District 2 race. It looks as though many of the local races are too close to call with 3,549 ballots officially counted.

There are still more than a thousand ballots left to count. Officials decide to begin the final counting process in the morning, as media members pick through the results of Montezuma Creek and Monument Valley.

Two votes for Willie Grayeyes – one for Kelly Laws in the results from Montezuma Creek. It brings the unofficial count of the District 2 commissioner race to 600 for Laws and 449 for Grayeyes.

When the votes for Monument Valley are counted, Grayeyes takes a 764-629 lead over Laws.

Phil Lynman holds 3,082 votes with three of the seven counties reporting results, not counting San Juan County. His opponent, Lisha Hall, stands at 1,116.

The results in San Juan County come in with Lynman leading 2,380-1,520. Lynman now has an unofficial 5,462-2,636 lead. It's one of a few races that can safely be called at the time. Kenny Maryboy and Adam Bruce are clearly headed for new terms.

Bruce ran unopposed for the retention of his commission seat. Maryboy holds a 537-366 lead over the "write-in" as it's written on the unofficial results spreadsheet.

All write-in candidates are totaled in one number and later sorted out. Andy Clarke is the only write-in candidate running against Maryboy.

During the Primary Election, it took three days to get the official results after the final ballots were cast. That prospect increasingly seems to be destined to repeat itself, as the minutes slowly tick away.

Officials await the arrival of Pugh from Navajo Mountain as it nears midnight. The night is coming to an end and it becomes clear it will be a few days before a winner is decided for the District 2 commission seat.

Nielson and Francom are back to work in the morning to count the remaining ballots, along with all the staff who have put in countless hours of work during the election season.

The prospect of change

The remaining mail-in ballots are still in the same place they were the night before. Francom is busy early. He prints off the unofficial results in the clerk's office. The Navajo Mountain results are in. Francom says the next scheduled official release of results will be on Friday, Nov. 9.

After the Navajo Mountain results are tallied, Grayeyes still holds an 817-648 lead over Laws. All that remains to determine the race officially is mail-in ballots.

San Juan County and the nation await the results of the District 2. The morning following the first election with new districting still produces no definitive results.

The prospect of a Maryboy and Grayeyes victory would give San Juan County the first Navajo-dominant commission in its 138-year organized history in the state.

Not only that, but it would give Utah it's first non-white majority-controlled commission ever. A member of the Navajo Nation has also never chaired a county commission in San Juan County.

As the dust continues to settle, the clerk's office diligently works its way through the verification process throughout the course of Nov. 7.

The following day they begin to work their way through the remaining ballots, counting a total of 980 when it's all said and done. They can now safely call all the races.

All that remains to count are a small number of provisional ballots from Montezuma Creek and any mail-in ballots that are postmarked on or before Nov. 6. The clerk's office believes those remaining votes will not be enough to sway any of the races.

It's all over now. The canvas results are still to come in the following week, along with the official results that will be approved by the county commission.

Willie Greyeyes defeats Kelly Laws in the newly delineated District 2 by an unofficial margin of 805-900.
Kenny Maryboy defeats the write-in candidate Andy Clarke 1,005-594.

The new commission which will be in place when they are sworn in in January will be composed of Maryboy, Greyeyes, and current chair Bruce Adams.

Phil Lynman receives 2,999-1,824 against Lisha Hall in San Juan County in the race for Utah House of Representatives, District 73.

The new commission will be comprised of two Democratic

commissioners in Grayeyes and Maryboy, with Bruce serving as the Republican minority.

"I think the voice of the people has been made known at the ballot box, and I'll do everything I can to work with them and help them be successful commissioners," Bruce said of his new counterparts.

What happens now?

Despite the historic shift in the commission, there is still an unknown factor facing Grayeyes. In August, Federal Judge David Nuffer reinstated Grayeyes on the November ballot, ruling that he was deprived of his due process by county clerk Nielson.

Nuffer additionally ruled that an objection to Grayeyes's candidacy was not filed within five days after he officially registered to run. Nuffer also stated that Nielson acted contrary to the law when he used a voter challenge to invalidate Grayeyes's candidacy.

The Lieutenant Governor's office was not in attendance at the August ruling and letters from local residents urging the office to investigate Grayeyes' legitimacy as a candidate have already begun being sent just days after his victory.

It was suggested that any legal questions regarding the residency of Willie Grayeyes (who lists an address on Piute Mesa near Navajo Mountain as his primary address) be decided after the election by Nuffer.

Grayeyes contends he was born at the location and that his umbilical cord was buried at the site, establishing his residency according to Navajo tradition.

While the residency of Grayeyes has been questioned, he has served in a myriad of positions in San Juan County.

In the past, he has served in leadership positions for the Navajo Mountain Chapter, served as president of the Navajo Mountain Community School Board, and served on the Utah Resource Advisory Council for the Bureau of Land Management. Grayeyes is also the chairman of the board of Utah Diné Bikeyah and has been a vocal supporter of the original Bears Ears National

Monument designation.

In the 1980s, when the voting boundaries were adjusted after a similar lawsuit, Grayeyes was serving as president of Utah Navajo Industries and was involved in the process of creating the new districts.

"You have to be positive to achieve consensus," Grayeyes said after the election. "We will create conversations to hopefully change local attitudes toward Native Americans and our priorities. You have to be positive in order to get results."

When asked if the race with Laws was as close as he expected it to be, Grayeyes said, "I'm not a fortune teller. I'm just a normal guy, that's it."

For Maryboy, there is no question of residency surrounding his victory. This is the second time Maryboy has served as San Juan County Commissioner.

He was previously elected to the commission first in 2006, taking his oath in 2007 and serving until 2015. His brother, Marc Maryboy, was the first Native American commissioner in the state's history.

"Congratulations to the San Juan County Commission, which now accurately represents a Native American-majority voice," Marc Maryboy said, who is a founding board member of Utah Diné Bikéyah.

Maryboy encouraged the new commission to focus on providing social services to all citizens in an equitable fashion. He emphasized that San Juan County has historically neglected the needs of local Ute, Diné, and Paiute communities, that approximately 40 percent lack running water and electricity in their homes.

As the potential legal battle concerning Grayeyes looms on the horizon, for now, we have the first non-anglo dominated commission in Utah history. They will officially be sworn in this January."

* * * * * * * * *

As the weeks ebbed and flowed on, Charlie continued adjusting to the pressures and politics that existed in that time and space in the world. He did his best to give all sides a voice and accurately reflect the sentiment of what was at stake for the county, the country, and a race that had been held down for hundreds of years. For the first time, these downtrodden had gained power at one of the highest levels of state government.

It was a time of staunch inner reflection for himself as he tried to sort out what he was doing there and what part he had to play in it all. Charlie knew there was some part for himself to play in it all, so he tried to talk to both sides.

The side he failed to talk to was that of his estranged mother of his son, Aubrey. He buried himself so deep in work with a belief that if he worked hard enough and wanted good things enough they would happen. Charlie slowly drifted away from his young family and solely into his work.

He tried to call and talk to his young son, but rarely would Aubrey allow him to talk with Joyce who Charlie felt a million miles away from. He didn't know how to fix the situation. He tried to make plans with Aubrey to allow for Joyce and her to come visit the canyonlands he was so enchanted with now.

Aubrey was beginning to drift away from him silently. She started to feel as if she didn't need Charlie for any of the struggles and that she could do it on her own. She started to believe he cared more about work than his family— most of all her.

Aubrey saw the editor job in Monticello as another means for Charlie to perpetuate his wanderlust and run from her and his responsibilities. She cursed him for not being there with her in her hometown where she felt safe and protected by the proximity to her mother and extended family. Charlie understood this and didn't want to take anything from her, but tried to tell her the pain it caused him to be away from his son. To him, he was comfortable in uncharted territory where the only sanctuary was completely immersing himself in his work.

"I can't just come live in Wyoming and do nothing," he told her. "There's no work there in order for me to support you and Joyce. We've tried this before. It's never worked. Aubrey, I love what I'm doing."

They could never compromise on the subject and periods would ensue where they didn't speak for several weeks.

Charlie would tailspin into a deep depression where he drank himself to sleep at night, wondering if he would ever be a part of his son's life again. He began to resent the paper and the community for all the conflict occuring in his life. He couldn't understand why there was so much division in the world and why they had to fight over everything. This was both of their homes. This was also the temporary home of countless millions that come here to experience what was once the home of the ancient ones.

It was all a fight to call a place home and be able to live there and enjoy it before someone came along and told you to get the hell out. It could be for whatever reason; the color of your skin, the religious group you belonged to, your job, who you vote for.

Charlie was always the outsider wherever he went. There was no home for him in the world, he felt. There was no place he belonged where there wasn't somebody presiding over it who'd stolen it from somebody else first. The group who stole it from everybody else is commonly referred to as the "local" wherever Charlie went, even as the editor of the local community paper, he would always be an outsider to these people.

He tried to blend in the best he could, getting drunk as often as possible on 3.2% beer.

There was only one bar in the town of Monticello, Utah—which had long been a dry town on account of the Navajo Reservation due south of town. This is what Charlie was told by the proprietor of the only bar in Monticello, which had just opened its doors shortly before Charlie arrived on the scene.

Charlie believed it more along the lines that the Mormons who controlled everything there couldn't partake in alcoholic beverages and therefore wanted to deprive the rest of the population of such liberties.

"Utah is changing," Charlie would spout off after having too many watered-down Utah beers. "Not everybody here is Mormon now. One day we will outnumber you, mark my words. Salt Lake City is already like that. It won't be long now before all those tourists that go to Moab will get a collective idea in their heads and move there."

Nobody there wanted that to happen, so Charlie would continue to push the idea. He just knew someday the earth would be overrun in every place and the rural would be invaded as every-thing else had been invaded already. It was just a matter of time in his opinion.

"You can't cling to one place as home these days," he would say to the other patrons. "Mobility is the key in this day of age. If you don't move, then you're trapped, and once your trapped life is nothing but a set of routines."

Nobody cared what he had to say, so he took to the paper, exacting a kind of revenge on the community, pushing the xeno-phobia he perceived as far as humanly possible. He tried to make them feel uncomfortable with covering the hidden treasures that existed and locals wanted kept a secret.

He would plaster photos of hidden petroglyphs on the front page of the paper, disregarding the warnings he had received tell-ing him not to do these kinds of things.

Charlie was beyond caring as he sat home at nights, fixated on his young son and trying to force the world to make sense again one drink at a time.

"There has to be some form of infinite justice out there to it all," he would think to himself. "It can't all be this endless line of battles?"

It began to wear on him and the knowledge began to creep into his mind he couldn't stay there. The winter made its descent onto the desert, suffocating it with a thick white blanket of fresh snow. It didn't stop accumulating for months that year as Char-lie covered the pending court trial over Willie Garayeyes' election victory.

Charlie got the feeling something wasn't right and he invit-ed his boss to lunch to ask him if everything was kosher.

They met at the small diner and the publisher told Charlie that he had been fired from the nonprofit he'd founded. He asked him to keep it a secret from the community. This of course meant he could no longer afford to pay Charlie his wages as the editor, stating he would "be needing to resume his old position of editor again."

"What am I supposed to do?" Charlie asked, wondering out loud where he would go after centering his life in the desert for four months despite the lack of habitable dwellings and the absence of his young son.

He quickly felt everything he sacrificed was for nothing.

"You have an immense talent, Charlie," the publisher said to him. "There's going to be something for you. I'm sorry this happened and I will give you a few weeks to figure out what you're going to do. You don't have to pay me back the money I gave you to relocate here, we can call that even."

"Is there anything I can do, or is it something that I didn't do right?" he asked the publisher.

"I've been hearing things," he responded. "I take it that you smoke marijuana?"

"I do, it's legal just twenty miles from here and it is on the ballot here finally," Charlie responded.

"You have to be extremely careful with that here," the publisher said. "It's not like Colorado where they will let you have it. They will raid you here even for a small amount."

"It's on the ballot for medical, you know that," Charlie said. "I think it's going to pass."

"Even if it does pass, the state legislature will try to hold it up as long as possible," he said to Charlie. "I don't care or anything like that, but there have been some concerns raised to me about it."

Charlie just thanked the publisher and ate his sandwich at the little diner and thought about what he would do now given this revelation. He didn't have much money and detested the thought of moving back to Wyoming with his tail tucked behind his legs, especially after Aubrey had refused to even speak with him or let him speak with Joyce. He wanted nothing more than to make it work, but he also knew that it might cost him his relationships in the process.

"Is the paper for sale?" Charlie asked the publisher.

"Of course," the publisher said. "Two hundred thousand

dollars," he responded with little hesitation to the question.

Charlie began to seek capital needed to buy the newspaper, turning over every rock in search of support. He tried his friends, family, and then finally the bank. None of it worked or had any prospects of working. They all wished him luck as he racked his brain trying to come up with a way to secure enough money to acquire the publication. The idea dawned on him to get it through a contract with the county itself.

He began hatching a plan to go to the new commissioners with a proposal to save them money, considering they were paying an outside organization over $600,000 a year to promote the county. He knew this through the financial records.

Charlie worked up the courage and began to call the three commissioners one by one. He first pitched them on the prospect of his acquisition of the county newspaper. Each commissioner had a different agenda and Charlie tried to sell the idea of his purchasing the newspaper conducive on the fact of a mutual agreement the publication would handle the county's tourism advertising for one year, cutting the cost of that expenditure to one-third of its current cost to the local taxpayers.

They were all onboard or at least told Charlie they supported him. Charlie in turn promised he would hire locals from the reservation.

In reality, it benefited two of the commissioners if they got Charlie in as the publisher and owner of the only newspaper in the county. Charlie had taken a favorable stance to them during their campaign bids and gave them a fair shake during the aftermath of the election. Willie Grayeyes had a trial coming up at the end of January and Charlie continued his coverage of the election challenge, drawing national coverage of the bizarre shift in the political landscape in the four corner county of Utah.

Charlie continued his nightly torturing of the locals at the speakeasy. Asking them annoying questions about some of the local spots nobody wanted tourists to visit. They looked at Charlie as a tourist.

Charlie didn't stop exploring the region, going to Mesa Verde at the start of a government shutdown that was being reported as a national crisis over border security with Mexico and the influx of immigration that was taking place by residents of Central America who were traveling through Mexico in an attempt to gain entry into the United States via the Mexican border.

Mesa Verde was closed because of the shutdown and Charlie went to get a look at the famous cliff dwelling as a single park ranger guarded the entrance, informing Charlie the trails were closed, but there was a lookout he could catch a glimpse of the dwelling from.

He continued to study past writers and explorers who lived in the same area. He tried to read Desert Solitaire by Edward Abbey, then read the Monkey Wrench Gang. He read Jim Stiles and quickly struck up a rivalry with him, taking an opposite stance as Stiles in their ideology about what should become of Bears Ears as the new commissioners were in favor of turning the monument back to its original designation of over a million acres.

Thanksgiving came and went. Charlie visited Aubrey and Joyce, reuniting with his son for the first time in four months, minus the phone calls she would answer when he was not calling at ungodly hours, badgering her to some indecipherable purpose. He could not understand her, despite how hard he tried through his limited capacity to listen to something other than his desires.

Aubrey wanted Charlie to be a part of Joyce's life, but she was unwilling to let her beloved son out of her hometown. She believed the boy was better by her side while he was young and this little. The father of her son had become a visitor in their lives and she cried.

"I look at you now and know I have pushed you away from me," she said to him the night he arrived for Thanksgiving. "I had so many chances and I messed them up and now all we have is this. Is there any way to fix any of it, or is it too late now?"

Charlie looked into her eyes and knew it was over. He thought about the times she refused to let him speak with his son and knew that woman could never be his future, only his past. He knew he would have to leave her and it would be the hardest thing he'd have to do in his life. He hoped it wouldn't be a fight and the boy wouldn't be hurt through it. He cursed himself for his failures.

"It's never too late, Aubrey," he said to her. "We can do whatever we want in life together if we truly are together. Life is hard enough without us fighting each other."

For years, Charlie tried to balance his responsibilities as a father and provider with Aubrey's desires to live near her family. He tried with every intention of doing what he thought was right by her to please her. Over time she could not follow him and his wanderlust and need for adventure. That was the thing she used to tell him she was attracted to him for, his desire to see the world and travel to see it.

She wanted to travel, but never got away from the world that was comfortable to her. Outside of her comfort zone things were strange and unhinged. She couldn't control the things she was used to controlling. There was no comfort in the outside world for her as it was cold and useless to the world she had always known. For her, the way to live life was to stay in one place and get comfortable. All that moving around and shuffling was of no use to her, although she envied people like Charlie who got to see the world. She wished so badly she could do that, but accepted she never would and that that was ok. Instead, she lived those things through Charlie and the television, but knew he was moving away from her.

"I couldn't stay in Utah, Charlie," she said to him. "It was driving me crazy to be away from everything I ever knew. I had to leave, Charlie. There was no other way."

"You didn't have to leave, Aubrey," Charlie said. "You could have made it work. There was nothing I wanted more in the world than for you to try. I needed your help more than anything and you left me. I know I got into my work and wasn't always there."

"I never left you, I was there the entire way," she said looking into his eyes, he looked away. "I might not have been right there with you, but I was with you."

Charlie didn't believe a word she said and knew the end was at hand. He was always looking to the end or the beginning of things and thought he'd waited too long to put an end to it once and for all even though he'd tried for so long to keep the wheels turning. There would be a price to pay for the procrastination down the line and he knew it. The real price he would pay through the years, but he pretended to have an inclination of what he couldn't possibly fathom.

"We tried our hardest and did the best we could," he said. "Sometimes things are just too difficult to overcome and we have to face reality."

They had Thanksgiving together as a family for the "last time" as Aubrey put it. Charlie tried not to think of it like that, but rather as time spent together and was thankful for that. It did nothing for him to put a price on the moment and he had forever been trying to learn to enjoy the moment and live in the moment. It was a practice in futility often times for him as he would leave the present to be somewhere else other than where he was. It didn't make a difference to Charlie where he was just as long as it wasn't in Wyoming, even though he practiced with sincere intent to be in the present wherever he was.

In this moment, Charlie couldn't realize it would be nearly a year until he was with his son again. It would be the last time he and Aubrey were together and friendly. His life after this point would be marred by legal battles and a constant shuffling even he would fail to understand, but then there would come the great peace.

None of that mattered at the moment and they enjoyed each other's company, knowing in the morning all of that would change again. They would no longer have the basic things they took for granted in each other, and Joyce would no longer have his father present in his daily life. It was the consequence of their youthful embrace, premature in their hearts, suffering for their inexperience and lust. They, like many of their contemporaries, had no idea what they were getting themselves into when they decided to have a child. They simply wished for the best and went forward. They were both fools and the day would come when Joyce resented them both for their youthful ignorance and haste.

A snowstorm struck the next morning and Charlie held his boy one last time before they were to be separated for a year. He said his goodbye to Aubrey as she cried a few tears knowing this was probably it for good this time around and there would be no reconciliation as it was the end of their journey together, but the beginning of a larger fight for her independence she would come to hold Charlie as the burglar of.

"I love you, Charlie," she said to him. "Don't forget that. There's going to be a lot that happens to us and to Joyce. I don't want you to forget I do love you, and I will always love you because you're the father of our son, we had a life together. I wanted nothing more than for it to work out."

"The storm is coming in pretty hard now," he said to her, looking at the world turning white around them. "I've got to go, or I'll be stuck in a ditch somewhere. I love you too, Aubrey. Everything happens for a reason. Even if we have no idea what that reason is."

And with that, they were separated from each other. They would no longer be accountable for each other's happiness, or sadness. Now they were accountable to themselves and their son, but never to each other.

Charlie made the long drive back to the Canyonlands, contemplating what the future had in store for him as he knew change was coming that would make his old life unrecognizable. He had Christmas, then his birthday to look forward to, followed by the new year and the newspaper he was tasked with running. There would be new friends and old friends that resurfaced. There would be love and there would be happiness somewhere amongst it all. He knew things would never be like they were before.

He would never know what it felt like to be a family with Aubrey and Joyce again together. That was their future and there was nothing Charlie could do about it in the present moment, so he went forward confidently, hoping for the best.

The next morning: Alexander Gumm

Charlie got wind about Alexander from Facebook. He found Alex after watching the response to his first article online, a piece about an anti Donald Trump rally against building a border wall with Mexico. There was Alex, plastered on Facebook like the missing kid poster in Walmart, or the back of a milk jug like they used to do in the movies when Charlie was a child.

Mark Zuckerberg, who Charlie discovered lived on the island and was building a massive doomsday complex that ran miles underground, would have been ecstatic his product was working for such means.

Alexander was a young existentialist, seeking the supreme eternity that comes with Nirvana. He came to Kauai looking for enlightenment, or some sort of answer to it all. When Charlie talked to Alexander's mother on the phone, she was hopeful but doubtful he was still alive because she hadn't heard from him in over a year.

After all, what son in the world wouldn't let his mother know he was alive and well after such a length of time?

His father seemed to be a little more accepting of the fact that he hadn't heard from him for over a year now. He knew his son was either alive and not wanting to communicate with his parents, or he had simply met his end. He'd reached the point of not fearing it either way.

The family was from Maine and ran a hotel after retiring from the newspaper business and serving as the publishers of a local paper. His father, Ben, talked to Charlie for a few minutes before handing the phone off to his wife, Sally. The more Charlie talked to her the more he felt, as a father, that she just wanted to be able to have some sort of closure and get on with her life.

To Charlie, there was no pain in the world worse than being

torn from your son or daughter and not being able to help them.

John Krakauer wrote about an individual very similar to what Charlie imagined Alex Gumm to be like in the book 'Into the Wild.' Krakauer's book was one of Charlie's favorites and he even brought it with him to Kauai and read it just before coming across Alexander's story.

Alexander was a restless young man of 23 years who had a passion for music and had got himself mixed up in the L.A. music scene. He played guitar in a band there and would move back and forth between California and Maine in an attempt to make it.

It was hard for Charlie to imagine what it would be like to live in Maine while writing the story, having never been there. It was a foreign concept to him. He related it to the context of how Utah and Hawaii turned out to be when he got there and started to get to the heart of the communities.

When the story ran after a few days of intensive work, Charlie didn't know how it would be taken by the public. He was the new guy that nobody cared about because the new guys came and went like toilet paper on Kauai.

Charlie wanted to make a splash with an article that meant something and help some grieving parents get some closure, even if that meant finding out their son was gone forever.

Alexander's parents held out hope he was at the Buddhist temple on island, which Charlie went to on his second morning on Kauai by what his guide called, "a call to his true dharma." It was Shiva's temple and was called 'where heaven meets earth.' For Charlie It truly was where heaven met earth, but for the location only in his mind. He walked around the temple and observed what was going on outside of the temple. Inside, people sat lotus style immersed in meditation, praying with the guide that performed a water pouring ceremony. At the entrance of a temple, a giant golden cow stood guard glimmering in the morning sun.

Charlie's was told by a spiritual teacher who was curious as to why he was there this was not the way the Buddhists there functioned, that they would make Alex call his parents and let them know where he was if he was under their monastery.

Charlie quickly formed a timeline on Alexander's last known

locations and communications with the world, following his trail until it eventually went cold. He found Alexander last used his cell phone to call a charter taxi company. When Charlie called the number, nobody answered, so Charlie decided to drive to the location where the business was listed. The company headquarters was in a gated house in Lihue, a true Hawaiian town with a rich history.

A small Filipino man came out of the front doors and reluctantly greeted Charlie as he proceeded to tell him who he was, why he was there and asked if the man knew anything about the missing boy.

His reaction to Charlie was hesitant, as he perceived there was a twinge in the man's answers, there was a certain knowing about what had truly happened. He confided in Charlie there was a cruise ship that made harbor that day and he would have in no way given the boy a ride in his taxi service because he would have been near the boat harbor where the cruise ship would have just docked. That was his story.

It was odd to Charlie he said with such certainty he would have been in one place on that specific day a year ago. Charlie could hardly remember yesterday, so it came off as fabricated in his view.

He told Charlie he would, "get ahold of him if he found out anything after he had asked around."

That conversation convinced Charlie the owner knew something and that there was most likely nobody who would ever know exactly what happened, and that it was dangerous to be on a possible murder trail digging for information alone. With the constructed timeline, there was more work done on the missing person case than had been done by the local detectives in 12 months.

The article about Alexander ran on February 26, 2019, under the headline 'Family of Alexander Gumm look for answers.'

It read—

"Ben Gumm and Sally McLaren hold out hope their son has found what he was looking for. They last talked to him at a bus station in North Berwick, Maine prior to his departure to Kauai in February of last year. That was the last time the parents laid eyes on their son as he has been missing on the island since Feb. 24 of 2018.

"He said, 'can you give me a ride to the bus depot? I'm leaving Maine to go to Kauai,'" his mother recalls of their last conversation.

The 25-year-old Alexander McLaren Gumm headed to Kauai in order to seek enlightenment. It was a path that he "matter of factly" was set on, his mom says, clinging to the hope Alex is somewhere on the island and someone has seen him.

Gumm had taken a vow of silence from his parents, Ben and Sally, and possibly everyone prior to his departure. They say he began to withdraw from his social circles in his hometown in Maine, where he was living with his parents prior to leaving. He didn't talk much about why he was going to Kauai, or what he wanted to do when he got here, other than to say he was seeking enlightenment.

Gumm's cell phone records indicated that he last contacted two cab companies after staying at the Kauai Beach House Hostel for two days on Feb. 22-23, 2018. His last known call from his cell phone was placed to the Kauai Beach House Hostel on Feb. 24, 2018.

The staff at the hostel remembers Gumm as a quiet and introverted person who kept to himself before leaving after his two-day stay at the hostel. That's also how his parents describe Alexander, as a young man that kept to himself and frequented Los Angeles from the time he was 17, working odd and end jobs in Maine between trips to California. When in California, Gumm was in a band pursuing his lifelong dream of becoming a professional musician. Gumm is a vegan and does not use drugs or alcohol according to his parents. He has a distinguishing tattoo on the underside of his left forearm: the Kundalini Staff of Life.
Gumm made two calls between Feb. 22-23, 2018. One to the A-1 Lift, Kauai Taxi and Island Tours company at 5:08 p.m. on Feb. 22. The other call was to the Kauai Taxi on Feb. 23, at 1:03 p.m.

The owner of the A-1 Lift, Kauai Taxi and Island Tours company said he did not recognize the photo of Gumm and that the 'Pride of America' cruise ship had come into port by that evening and that he was not operating in the Kapaa region that night.

The Kauai Taxi company has no record of Gumm in their system and said the same cruise ship was in port that night and they were, "incredibly busy." The company said they would have most likely turned Gumm down for a ride, as they do not operate in Kapaa where the beach hostel is. They only operate in Lihue.

Gumm's parents believe he may have sought out either the Buddhist or Hindu monks on the island to perpetuate the knowledge he gained from an excursion to India. His mother Sally said that an investigation was opened by the Kauai Police Department (KPD) in March of 2018 and they have heard little from the detective who heads up the case.

"He did an extensive amount of research on Buddhism, spiritualism, on ascension, on enlightenment and the Bible," Sally Gumm said. "He was a big fan of Jesus Christ as a teacher and a healer. He did a lot of research on healing herbs and natural supplements...He loved the outdoors and was very interested in that. One thing he said about L.A. was, 'there's too much cement and not enough trees.' Kauai was right up his alley as far of the natural resources."

His parents, like any loving parents, don't understand if he is alive and well why he is not contacting them. All they can think of is if they came to the island looking for him that he would say, "what are you doing here?"
"He hasn't taken any money out of his bank account," his father said in an interview with the Garden Island. "We're connected with his cell phone records and so we're incredibly worried about him."

In a press release, the KPD said, "Gumm is reported as five feet, 11 inches tall, weighing approximately 160 pounds. He has brown hair and is of Caucasian descent.

He has a blue tattoo on his left forearm, approximately eight inches long, of a staff with energy spirals. Gumm has another blue tattoo on his right hand of the symbol of the third eye."

The article had a decent reception and was the most popular on the sleepy little daily newspaper's website that had been churning out newspapers since 1905 for one day. There were tons of sordid comments on the article and the parents received myriads of strange tips about possible sightings of their son.

One account even provided photographic evidence of a man who had wrapped himself in medical bandages as a sort of clothing breaking into their home when they were away for food. The mother and father kindly informed the woman, who reached out to them after reading the article, that it couldn't possibly be their son because their son was not a thief.

Another account had the boy recognized by the distinctive tattoo on his wrist as a positive confirmation that it was indeed Alexander. The woman who reached out to Ben and Sally was a woman who brought food to the homeless that lived in Salt Pond on the west side of the island where it was considerably drier and warmer than the other parts of the island. When the woman offered this man some corn chowder, he politely denied her, despite the obvious fact he was starving. The man with the tattoo politely told the woman he could not eat the corn chowder because he was a vegan and asked if she had some almonds instead, that he would be forever grateful if she had any.

The woman did not have any almonds and the young man shrugged it off and went back about his way, seeking enlightenment.

This possible Alexander sighting was followed by another in Salt Pond where someone identified a young man that matched Alex's description as having been indoctrinated by a cult who were reshaping a young man down by the docks with some food, offering it to him if he followed their ways. When the young man would stop listening, or wouldn't submit to what he was being told, the food was withdrawn.

It started to look more and more like Alex was in the Salt Pond area and Charlie made it a priority to find him for his parents after a detective called him and attempted to pry information off Charlie. In addition to farming Charlie for his intel, the detective informed him if the boy was located, he would be detained and institutionalized before he could be released.

That bit of information terrified Charlie to the core.

"If they can lock that poor bastard up in a nuthouse for going off grid, they can do it to any of us," he said to Daniel in the newsroom one day. "It's a crime to renounce the world apparently and the authorities need to evaluate your sanity if you do it. What the hell is the world coming to?"

"They've been trying to do it for years," Daniel responded. "It's no different than it's always been. Your boy probably went hiking in the Kalalau Valley and fell off a cliff. The pigs found him first, end of story."

As time went on and the first weeks and initial rush of the island faded behind Charlie, he told himself he was the only one who could find the young man and that when he did, he would bring some almonds for the young enlightenment seeker.

Charlie felt for Alex's parents and he could feel their pain through the phone as they just wanted to know what happened to their son.

"If they could only have some damn closure," he thought to himself, "then maybe they could have a chance of moving on with their lives and putting whatever happened behind them."

Charlie advised the parents they needed to find a good man to track Alex down and that he didn't know any. He didn't want them to think that he was trying to profit off Alex going missing or anything like that so he decided to let it go. After all there was always more news coming his way daily now, more than he knew how to handle.

In May, Charlie was at Salt Pond Beach Park listening to Henry Noa's speech to local Hawaiians about annexing land and retaking the Kingdom of Hawaii from the occupier, the United States of America through physically occupying land. Near the end of the speech Charlie got up to walk around the crowd. A local man came up and shook his hand.

"Thank you for being here," he told him as they made small talk about the Salt Pond. He told Charlie Alex helped take care of the sacred sold ponds there and helped the man's family in making the pink salt.

"Have you seen him around today?" Charlie asked the man.

"Yeah, he lives with us," he said. "He's a cool guy, he works and takes care of his business and stays to himself. His family was just tripping out, so we gave him a phone and he called his mom and told her he was fine."

Charlie never told Alex's family about the encounter he had with a man that confirmed Alexander was living at the Salt Pond until some time later when articles appeared in the New York Post and UK Daily Mail when Charlie had left the island for his young son.

A group of Alex's friends went looking for him on the island for six days almost a year after Charlie had written the article, making a documentary about their missing friend and getting almost every factual detail wrong in their search. They hiked into the Kalalau trail and almost drowned before leaving one of their party marooned behind on the trail with a possible concussion and an 18-mile hike out.

They still haven't located Alexander to this day and Mark Zuckerberg still lives on the island despite buying up 700 acres of sacred Kuleana lands to create his doomsday resort.

Charlie's Kauai Landing

As Charlie sat in the Los Angeles airport, awaiting his flight and getting properly soused at an overpriced airport bar, the pull of Kauai began to tug in its intensity. When he'd left San Juan County, the island grabbed ahold of him from afar and began to pull in an unmistakable direction towards her.

On the threshold of taking the flight to get to the island, Charlie got a feeling this was one of the best things to ever happen to him. It was the possibility there could be some kind of sanity in America and hope was still alive for something amazing. That there actually existed a true paradise in what he had heard called the greatest nation in the world his entire life. He didn't know yet if it really was.

Some Hawaiians on Kauai were angry for being robbed of their Kingdom, unjustly by a confused and land-hungry "manifest destiny" thirsty nation 125 years before. Charlie was making the move to the Hawaiian island he had dreamed of for so very long after failing at other paradises. He had no clue what Hawaii had to offer outside of the typical stereotypes of lei's and hulas and all that generic unauthentic iconoclastic cultural norms that are assimilated in one's mind throughout the course of a lifetime.

Charlie was going to Grover Cleveland's lost chance to right America and steer her ship to the way of a truly righteous national character. The Hawaiian Kingdom, which achieved one of the world's highest literacy rates at one point, was now illegally annexed in the eyes of a growing movement there. They looked upon the haole presence more and more as an illegal occupation that had lasted for over 125 years.

The anger was palpable from the kanaka maoli and the movement was starting to grow with each passing day. Charlie was headed straight into the heart of it.

He felt guided and pulled there with an undeniable magnetic strength. Or perhaps it was just movement and nothing else. It was better to believe it all had some kind of cosmic meaning and was moving towards something of great significance.

The radar over Kauai showed a spinning mass of clouds about 50 miles off the coast. "Fuck it," Charlie thought as the cocktails went down smoother and more expensive at the airport bar in Los Angleles and he loosened up. He met a woman who was on the same flight as he was.

She started to tell him tales of her experiences on Kauai. They needed to have a cigarette which was near illegal in Tupac's state that somehow now turned into the land of entitled hipsters who cared more about their clothing than good conversation and actuality.

"Good thing I'm getting the hell out of this godforsaken state," Charlie told himself with an audible voice.

A man who'd just flew back from an extended trip in Papua New Guinea and told grand tales of his time there, convinced Charlie to accompany him (with their female companion) to the international terminal, the only place in the airport that had a smoking lounge. The man handed them both freshly minted coins from Papua New Guinea as he shared pictures and his excitement about going home to sleep in his own bed that night.

"Only people catching international flights are allowed to smoke in Los Angeles nowadays," the man said to Charlie and the woman. "It kind of makes you wonder what the world is coming to."

The man was flying back to Canada and the woman was on the same flight to Kauai as Charlie, headed there for the fifth time in her life. The woman tantalized Charlie with tales of Kauai and what he was heading into.

They had an hour before both of their respective flights and they hustled to the international terminal, catching a shuttle to the separated buildings. The woman, who Charlie refused to get her name, started to panic they would not make it back to the gate in time to catch their flight to the westernmost of the Hawaiian islands besides Niahau, the forbidden island. As they got out to the outdoor terrace, filled with people from all over the world, Charlie started to speak in Spanish as he was prone to do when the inebriation kicked in and he got tired of boring conversation.

Charlie talked to a couple from Mexico about how the United States was creating a fake border crisis to serve the current administration's need to create fear and stir up their base. But started to speak English when his Spanish failed to express what he was trying to get across in the conversation.

"It's complete insanity and people are actually buying this bullshit," Charlie told the couple. They nodded in agreement.

"I went down there a few weeks ago," he said, slurring words. "There was nothing there but a good time and the good old exploitation of a culture by gringos looking to do cocaine and get as many hookers as possible."

The couple laughed it off as a joke, but knew all too well what he meant.

Charlie's compadres were ready to leave him by this point, so he grabbed all his hurriedly packed stuff and hastened to catch his flight into a dry hurricane. He knew it was going to get messy, but that didn't matter, this was just the beginning.

"If I have to fly into the island on the tails of a small hurricane, then to hell with it," he told the man from who had just got back from Papa New Guinea before wishing him best of luck on his travels and thanking him for the coin.

Seven hours later and sitting next to the girl who he still refused to grab her name, the flight landed in a headwind of 110 knots. Charlie talked to the pilots and thanked them after the landing.

They were both white as ghosts.

Puerto Penasco:
Viva la Mexico

Charlie and the publisher were finishing up the paper. It was unusual they worked together this late, let alone worked together at all.

Most of the staff were gone for Christmas break, so he and the publisher were the last working to put out the paper, forced out of necessity to do things other people normally did. One of those things was design the paper.

Charlie's boss hemmed and hawed about how he would design the paper, but as they got closer to the deadline in the morning, it became clear Charlie would have to do it. The front page photo normally was one somebody sent in capturing the beauty of the landscape in the Four Corners. It was a photographer's dream there.

When you walked out into the desert night and gazed at the vastness of the imminent universe beating down on the very depths of your soul, it made an impression on the inner photographer. The longer you lived there, the more you tended to try and capture the stark beauty of the red rocks and slicked canyons through a camera.

Christmas week in a deeply religious Utah town sent Charlie searching for the usual photo submissions for the front page. The usual quintessential sunset or sunrise photo wasn't there for the go-to front-page picture he usually relied on. On Christmas day, which was three days passed now, Charlie went to Bears Ears National Monument to roam the land, finding his first self discovered petroglyphs by accident. Something he likened to a religious experience he tried to tell people about, but nobody listened to.

Charlie's son and mother Aubrey were supposed to visit and

spend the holiday with him, but it fell through. The holiday was to be spent alone, utterly crushing Charlie to miss Christmas with his three-year-old son and estranged love. Joyce loved ripping the wrapped presents to shreds. Knowing he was going to miss that, he knew there was nobody else to blame but himself.

He could leave it all behind and go back to his family, he thought. The stubbornness kicked in and he killed that thought.

When Charlie awoke to Christmas morning without his young family and a keen knowledge his entire relationship was falling apart, he had to do something tangible other than drink on the finest of holidays celebrating the birth of Jesus.

"There's more to do today than kill myself with the feelings that palgue me," he tried to tell himself.

A day bag was packed and Charlie headed out the door and into that anciently traveled Indian Creek unit of Bears Ears. It was his favorite place in San Juan County so far, having been in the famed county for just over two months.

He wrote an account about his Christmas experience in the paper the next week, bringing Elvis's "Blue Christmas" out of the bag, using it as a reference to the loss of the monument to Trump's redesignation. It was about his exploration that day in Indian Creek and finding his first petroglyphs there.

The first petroglyph he found was of an antelope. A single petroglyph on an impressive sheer red rock that had crashed off the face of the straight up and down Slickrock cliff, towering a hundred yards overhead. The petroglyph itself had been vandalized as somebody circled it and inscribed their names and the date of their "discovery."

It was the first time Charlie had come face to face with the desecration so many of the locals and natives talked about.

After he found the first one, there was a spark of inspiration as he kept moving along the bottom of the canyon and kept finding more petroglyphs, and eventually a panel that is still the biggest collection outside of Newspaper Rock.

A little way beyond the panel Charlie saw a rock that had been split in half by time. On it was what he believed to be an Anasazi spiral, taking up the better part of the rock face. To Charlie, that experience was one of the most spiritual things to be felt by a human being. To be able to stare at something another created, presumably thousands of years prior and know you are standing in the exact same spot, all this time in between.

He took a picture of that rock in the early morning Christmas sun and plastered it on the front page of the paper that week. A move he knew was bound to piss some of the staunch locals who believed showing people the petroglyphs and ruins that dotted the landscape would entice others to come in droves. Then the desecrations would follow and the trashing of the land, which had been happening more and more with the increase of visitation.

It was estimated over ten million people flowed through the region every year. The winter offered an escape, beautiful and to be held in awe, from the crowds of tourists. But as the winter progressed, Charlie felt the discontent within the scope of his life and the political tragedies that existed within the county and nation.

He needed a vacation.

As he and his boss finished the paper that had a sacred petroglyph photographed on the front page, Charlie's boss started to get calls from his wife. She was wondering when he was coming home because they had company over. The company consisted of two elders of the Mormon church. Charlie's boss was a Mormon, living in the heart of Utah in peace where his ancestors had founded the very town he owned a newspaper in. There was a long line of history there that Charlie dared to never understand.

He invited Charlie to dinner with his family and these elders of his church. The elders were living in town on a mission for the Church of Latter-Day Saints, who had recently decreed not to call or be called Mormons any longer, but rather "LDS." The decree was made by their new president Russell M. Nelson, who is 96-years-young and still skis and speaks fluent Spanish.

Charlie's polite decline of the dinner offer did not satisfy his boss, as he demanded Charlie join them for dinner and not spend the evening alone. It was after reading Charlie's editorial the week before that he thought Charlie was deeply depressed and felt it necessary to extend the offer considering he was the one who had brought Charlie there in the first place.

"Maybe some of it will rub off on Charlie," his boss thought to himself. "Religion never hurt anyone who didn't have it coming to them."

Charlie knew all too well that it would turn into some religious topic where they tried to convert him to wear magic underwear. It's what made him decline the offer in the first place. It was easy for him to foresee, so the attempt to head it off and not let it evolve into that kind of thing was made.

For Phil Boyle, he was not going to be denied the right to try and convert an invalid to the kingdom of heaven and eternal salvation. He was going to have Charlie over to make pizzas and convert him to Mormonism "by golly" if it was the last thing he did on God's green earth. It would have been an ordeal to tell him no for the second time, so Charlie was forced to take him up on the offer and they went to his new house on the hill he had just finsihed the construction on. It was Phil's crown jewel for all the work he had done for the community over the years at the paper.

But as they went inside the beautiful new home and took their coats off and were embraced by his lovely wife, their kids and the plump elders, there was a genuine warmth that could be felt. It was the loving grace of a family happy to have their father back and it was not the usual grind of politics and the paper, but was on a different level that made it human and more connectable for Charlie as a person.

They made their pizzas and talked about things. Charlie's conversation with his son and daughter was pleasant and centered around things like school and plans with school, only the boring stuff.

As the night wore down, Charlie informed them he planned to drive to Mexico in the morning. That he wanted to see this border situation himself.

"Be safe," Phil said. "There's a chance Trump will close the border while you're down there."

"I don't think they can just close the border like that on a whim, Phil" Charlie responded.

"Just make sure that you take care of yourself down there and if they are about to close the border, you get out of there as fast as you can," Phil said. "If you get into any trouble you can always call me."

Charlie thanked him for the courtesy and reminded himself he would likely not be there if he called him and that it was just a formality, but polite and thoughtful nonetheless.

The thought Phil believed the border could just be closed like that with an executive order was troubling to Charlie. Phil was a man who was the publisher of the only newspaper in a 712 square mile county that was genetically Republican and feared such a thing happening. Charlie knew better. He knew that it was all a bunch of hot air to stir up the base and pander to the fears of people who had never actually been to Mexico, but knew of its evils.

"Goodbye Phil, thanks for having me over and don't worry, I speak Spanish, so I should be ok, I think," Charlie told him as he headed out the door into the snow-packed high desert December evening, getting lost in the mountains where Phil lived when he drove away, taking a wrong turn on his way home. He made it home eventually and loaded a small bag for the morning, then got bored and went to the bar to take in his birthday at midnight. A tradition that he'd become accustomed to every year for sometime now.

The age of 32 had a ring to it for Charlie.

"It would have been nice to get to spend it with my son, who I had made arrangements to spend it with, but his mother flaked out on meeting me. She told me that 500 miles was far too far to drive and that if I wanted to see him and spend my birthday, I would have to drive up there and see him," he told a friend who called him to wish him a happy birthday. "It would have been the third time driving up there in recent weeks and it didn't dawn on her that I had to work and couldn't get away as easily as she could, but no matter how I reminded her of this, she refused to come to see me and I'm starting to see the writing on the wall."

None of that mattered, he forced upon himself. Down the hatch the drinks went, one after another. The music started to get better and time flowed on in good fashion. The hour eventually struck midnight with rapid succession as friends were made and

Charlie declared, "It's Mexico or bust for me boys, better take a shot with me, for tomorrow I will be in Trump's promised land."

They we're all staunch Republicans who adored the idea of a wall going up between Mexico and the United States.

Charlie had gotten into many arguments over the very tenuous subject with the local patrons who frequented the speakeasy which served as the only bar in the once dry town.

"Fuck those Mexicans, make them come in legally," one guy named Chad would tell Charlie.

"If you build that damn wall, you're going to have to tear down the statue of liberty you know?" he said to the bearded fellow, who was married to one of the uptight bartenders at the bar who Charlie terrorized nightly. "You're going to have to chisel out what's written on her and then demolish the fucking thing if you build that idiotic wall."

"You're a libtard and I'll kick your ass," the bearded one would usually say before they settled on drinking another round and getting aggravated over things they both couldn't control. The owner and bartender, a Mormon fellow named Ken, bought the speakeasy with his wife the previous year. Neither of them drank, so they thought it made perfect sense to open a bar and watch all the people who do drink get as drunk on 3.2 percent beer as humanly possible.

They had a cattle prong behind the bar for protection against any unruly behavior that may compromise their morals or character. They would show it off and use it on volunteers who weren't phazed by the jolt of electricity. The owners were nice people for the most part and would on occasion give Charlie a ride to his house when he'd had a few too many.

"The problem with the Mormon church is that you guys just want to get into our pockets and take everything for your cause or hungry gods," he would tell Ken, always practically yelling in his ear. "You see that golden statue next to the temple? It's hard for me to believe the Mormon church is composed of Christians when there is a golden statue outside their place of worship. Isn't that against Christianity or something, to make a golden statue in the church and worship it?"

"It's not against the Christian church to have golden statues, look at the Catholic Church," he said soberly to Charlie.

"You've got a point there, but still," he conceded. "What do you think would happen if I took my samurai sword and cut it in half? Do you think I would get life in jail? Or would they execute me on the spot, no trial or nothing, just straight to the execution?"

"Yes," he said before dropping Charlie off at his house. Charlie went in and packed a few last items for his trip, stumbling about as he said a prayer to get to Mexico in one piece and alive, before he called it a night, fading into that desert star filled evening with the excitement of a million cervezas dancing in his head.

When the morning came, time was taken to move slowly and be as mentally prepared as possible before leaving. The drive was 615 miles and would take over ten hours for Charlie to get there. He was going to do it in one day. It was a feat of endurance, but Charlie had done long distances of this sort frequently of late and had grown a strange unnatural fondness for the road. It was mostly his love of freedom and having the highway all to himself with his thoughts actively on the move throughout the world that he loved so much.

The Bears Ears peaked out through the desert, just visible to Charlie. They are a small doubled hill that isn't even in the national monument after the new designation, but bears the name. Charlie passed Blanding, the dry town where the FBI raided locals by gunpoint less than a decade ago.

Allegedly, they were looking for stashed artifacts families had acquired through the generations. The informant who ratted all the locals out committed suicide after the raid, along with a family physician who had birthed many of the residents.

Bluff passed by with its sign that reads "Founded in 800 AD" with the Twin Rocks Cafe greeting motorists under the famous Twin Rocks that stand out in defiance, bold and jagged, vibrant and red. It was a town that had just incorporated and already aimed its sights at attracting as many tourists as possible with new hotels and things they deemed to be desirable for tourists such as brightly colored eateries.

It was inhabited by an ultra-liberal subset of a few hundred that wanted to create a utopia on the banks of the San Juan River where the weather is always pleasant and they only get a few inches of snow a year.

South of Bluff lies the famous Monument Valley and the Mexican Hat which were covered in a fresh snow. A two-lane highway zips you past the iconic rock structures before casting you deep into the Navajo Nation, eventually arriving at Kayenta and Tuba City before ascending into Flagstaff.

Then it was into Camp Verde and the outskirts of Phoenix for Charlie on his journey, catching the Arizona 85 on a straight path to the border, dipping through Ajo and the Mexican American town of Why, which is unlike anything else he could recall being in.

The night silhouetted the Organ Pipe Cactus National Monument as Charlie marveled at the famous cacti that give the monument its name. There was nothing more to do but to stop and wander through that anomaly of nature which seemed surreal, but existed right then and there. The thought crossed his mind it wasn't safe to stop, especially with all the military and government around because of the shutdown over the wall. He talked himself out of going into the monument on foot and told himself he would try again on the way out when the sun was up.

National Public Radio had been informed Charlie was there as a kind of a serious joke and he offered his services after working with them a few weeks before. They were not interested, or at least that is what Charlie took from it, but he wanted to try and document the situation in some way to practice for when NPR did want him to do something for them. He knew deep down that day would never come, but he wanted to make himself feel important like he was on some kind of mission.

When he got to the border, pure madness played out in circus fashion before him. Not in the sense people were trying to get in illegally, but in the sense of the tension and feeling that existed there. The border guards gave Charlie looks beamed with ice-cold intensity that could be felt at all times. There was no place to escape it. When he got to the actual border crossing, a camera came down and took a picture of Charlie and his vehicle before he was moved forward in livestock fashion through the crossing where two Mexican officials looked at him through their post in his 1999 Honda Civic, the greatest piece of shit Charlie ever owned. When he pulled out his passport and tried to talk to them, they told him, "no esperate," setting Charlie free into one of his favorite nations in the world.

The lovely border town of Sonoyota greeted Charlie and he had to tell himself to drive normal, that there was nothing different here, it was the same rock, the same kind of road, in the same car. It was all just something to take in as he watched the people go about their nightly routine. The complicated simplicity of it all is what Charlie loved about Mexico. He also frequently told people that Mexico has the best beaches in the world.

It was his 32 birthday and he was pulling into Mexico at 9:15 p.m. on a Saturday in the prime of his life with a pocket full of cash. It was going to get messy, but first he had to secure lodging for the evening. He had the problem of no cell phone service on account of being in a different country, so he drove to what looked like the beach strip and tried to locate the hotel he'd looked up with rudimentary map skills.

His plan quickly failed, so he went to the main drag where all the bars and street people were hustling and pulled up to a spot and snuck up on a taxi driver.

"I'll give you ten bucks if you take me to the Playa Beach Hotel," he said to a man sitting in a taxi, pulling out the bill to let him know he meant business. He looked at Charlie stunned for a second.

"I don't know that hotel," he told him. "But I can take you to a place where there are hotels."

They agreed to do business and Charlie went to his car as two hustlers came up on the deal from the street to see what was happening. They asked Charlie if he wanted something.

"Solo pura vida primos," he told them.

Charlie fired up the Honda Civic without a muffler and the two hustlers flashed a sign of approval, nodding at him as he pulled out behind the taxi and followed him for about two miles until the taxi signaled to turn down a street.

Charlie missed the turn and was forced to do a u-turn in a place he had no business doing one, almost hitting a few cars in the process. The taximan nodded at him in a sign of approval as he took a right down the street that was so generously recommended.

It was like any other touristy drag in Mexico. It had all the essentials a gringo would ever need while in-country.

There were strip clubs everywhere, liquor stores, clubs that had no people in them and of course, Charlie's personal favorite, the street hustlers who offered you everything you could ever want to die from. The negotiations were always critical for Charlie when dealing with these kinds of individuals. He knew they, just like you, were always looking for the best deal and a way to make a few easy bucks.

This was easy to understand for Charlie and he always tried to remember it was all a negotiation and all things are negotiable and for sale, except when they wanted to rob and or kill you. Then things were out of your control and it was all over. The key here for Charlie was to not get in that kind of situation and have a good birthday night.

None of the hotels looked inviting to him, except the one at the end of the road that shined with a golden hue. It spoke to him saying, "Come here and have a golden sanctuary on the beach."

Strolling into the reception, an elevated bar stood out in all its glory, offering Charlie up the opportunity to have a few drinks before heading out into the dark Mexican night. The possibilities were limitless and the price of the hotel was modest, making it a win all around. It was still early, so he grabbed the important things from the car, making sure it was safe in the place it was parked and that it wouldn't be unceremoniously stripped down to the frame.

There were still two hours left in his birthday, so he didn't stop when passing the elevated bar, seeing as nobody was there, heading out into the depths of the strip, going into whatever the night had brought him over 600 miles for.

This was the first time he'd gone to Mexico alone. All the times prior were with a group and it was always the majority rule who made the decisions. When you travel alone, you have the freedom to walk about and decide what you want to do at your own pace. He knew the pace of the evening was going to be frenetic when three women and one guy walked past him, stumbling and heading back to the safety of their rooms before the street people ate them alive.

They were sitting ducks in a situation like this and there wasn't much to do other than watch. They attracted the dregs of the underworld with the way they walked at night. They didn't get 10 yards before a street guy appeared out of the darkness and asked them very audibly, "You look so beautiful, now how can we make this a night to remember?"

The group of three didn't say a word to the man, but picked up their pace and continued in the direction of the hotel, seeking the fine comforts that could only be found there for them in this setting.

I felt sorry for the guy who was just trying to supply a much-needed demand that comes with the night. He was walking in the same direction as Charlie and he had an inkling the man knew the real story of how the place functioned.

"Hola me calle amigo," Charlie said to him, lighting up a cigarette.

"Can I have one of those man?" he responded.

"Sure thing," Charlie said, handing him one while slowing down his pace to walk next to him. "What was those three's problem?"

"They're uptight, they only know how to have one kind of fun." he said to Charlie, lighting up the cigarette he had given him.

He was a short man. Probably not much taller than five feet, but had an air about him making him of a larger stature than he was. He possessed a devilish smile. One of those you can see from a mile away and know the meaning of, but still be enticed into being tricked by.

"What is there to do around here?" Charlie asked. "It's my

birthday and I don't want to mess around and get straight to what this place is all about. I've never been here before and probably never will be again, so this is the night my friend."

"Happy birthday amigo, how old?"

"32," Charlie responded.

"I just turned 31," the man said to Charlie, who looked him over, baffled the man was younger than him. He looked like he was in his 50's to Charlie.

He proceeded to tell Charlie prostitution was the main cup of tea around town and all the clubs offered it. He was intimately familiar with many of them, having spent most of his time hustling and chasing women there.

"Half of them never gave me the time of day until I became their pimp," he said to Charlie, leading him up the stairs to an establishment advertising ice-cold beer and women. It was a combo that went together with the name of the place — "The Blue Lizard."

Charlie went upstairs with the man who went by the name Chi-Chi as he greeted people along the way. They sat down at an empty table and ordered a few beers, on Charlie of course.

Chi-Chi told Charlie he knew all the girls there and that he could get him to dance with any of them he wanted.

"Any of them," he said. "Or all of them at the same time? It's your choice amigo, the world is your oyster."

It was never Charlie's thing to get involved with strip joints or women of the night. He preferred meeting women in some kind of semi-social circumstance, then dating them for years before it became some good old fashioned war where the walls caved in. That was how he liked it — to be miserable and content all at once. He wouldn't have things any other way.

"I'm not really into it amigo, but if this is what's going on tonight, then I am always down to go with the local style," Charlie said, receiving an ice-cold Mexican beer that hit the spot perfectly.

"You see the one over there? She used to be my girlfriend and I know her very well," Chi-Chi said, pointing out a girl that looked like she could be 16 at most. "I can get her to give you a dance if you would like?"

Charlie looked at her for a minute and knew there was no way he would ever go any further than a dance with one of these women of the night, so he told him that out of honesty.

"No thanks."

"It's all good primo," he responded to Charlie's declaration against women of the night, smiling and laughing at the same time. "You can always change your mind after a few drinks."

They had a series of drinks after that. One after another they put them down until the music started sounding better and a group of Europeans came over and hugged Chi-Chi, thanking him for setting them up with the girls on their last trip.

They sat with the group, many of them were from Ireland, there on vacation like Charlie. They were there to get drunk and have as much fun as possible before heading back to the drudgery of their lives, but here they were attempting to enjoy the moment.

Chi-Chi informed Charlie he had to go do a deal and would not be back. He thanked him for the beers and offered him some cocaine. Charlie declined, but Chi-Chi insisted he take some because he was offering it for free and as a gift and if he declined the offer, that was considered rude and unacceptable.

"If you insist that I take some of your cocaine, sir, then I shall take what you offer me," Charlie told him, now partially inebriated and getting closer to drunk by the second. "But if I take said cocaine, I insist that you take some with me here and now because I am sketched out with all this fentanyl situation that's been killing people. One of my friends died in Vegas not that long ago. My dead friend bought what he thought was a bag of coke, but it ended up being spiked with that shit and he went into a coma and died."

"That's heavy compadre, but I will absolutely do some with you," he said. "But I warn you, senor, this is some good shit. It will make your birthday night more interesting, this I can guarantee you."

And with that, he handed him what appeared to be a loose produce bag, tied up with a small twisty. Chi-Chi used his keys to break through the package into the white powder that controls so much of the world and is responsible for much of the evils. He then handed it to Charlie, who was relieved he was taking some of his own stash, showing Charlie he wouldn't die from it.

Charlie thanked him and headed back into the dregs of the night, just as he was when he had met Chi-Chi. Charlie wandered the streets in search of something better and before long found even better strip joints that buzzed with loud music and lights that entranced. There were only strip joints to choose from and Charlie felt it imperative to choose the right one, or else his birthday night would be even worse than it was now, running to Mexico from Aubrey who wanted to steal his soul as he felt she was trying to do.

So he turned into one of the establishments that looked decent enough to spend some time in without dying. It was full of older Americans, many couples there together enjoying a nice strip dance. He sat at a table alone and ordered a drink, marveling at the couples, and how they could do this together. There was literally zero chance Aubrey would ever do a thing like that with him and he envied the couples who were there for their ability to let go and have some fun, or at least do something different and try to make the best out of the situation.

The lights went down and the best of the best dancers in Puerto Penasco made their way onto the stage, displaying all their dazzling features, or what they deemed to be attractive to all those in the audience who gazed intently as their clothes slowly came off in liquid movements.

Charlie ordered another drink and started to get sloppy in his approach.

One dancer pulled a guy up on stage and then the guy's girlfriend joined them as they all slowly lost their clothes and started to have sex on stage, but not before dry humping for a measurable amount of time that seemed to go on and on in endless agony.

The sloppiness increased as Charlie turned away from the grotesque sight, knowing this was the best it was going to get that night and he would have to deal with another year of failures such as these and just keep trying until one day he found something that was so amazing he would instantly become jaded from it and dislike it as well.

When he'd had his fill and was over the only entertainment offered in Puerto Penasco, the feeling rushed over him he was destined to walk the streets late at night. The vulnerability of it made Charlie consider an alternative and he looked around the club and saw some younger gentlemen arguing with other people at another table.

When he went there to see what was happening, it was apparent the two younger gringos sitting at a table together and doing most of the arguing, had no clue what they were doing or the trouble they could get themselves into.

"The car won't start and we have to get out of here," one of them said to the other as they looked at each other nervously. "We can't leave the car here overnight or it will be on blocks by the time we get here in the morning."

"You tried to start it, didn't you," the other responded.

"I did, but the damn battery is out of juice or something like that, and these assholes at the next table better stop talking shit or somebody is about to get murdered," the older looking one said.

"Hola amigos," I said. "I couldn't help but overhear your troubles and I think I might have a solution for you."

"Who the fuck is this guy?"

"I'm Charlie Porter, a local weirdo like yourselves just enjoying my evening at this fine Mexican strip club. Let me buy you guys a drink and then we'll figure this whole thing out."

After a few drinks, Charlie discovered the two were brothers who'd moved down from Arizona after running into some hard times with the law. They fled to Mexico with a dream of living the simple life, but were too young to pull it off. You could tell by the way they spoke, they lived an entitled way of life as if anywhere they went was lucky to have them grace the place's presence.

They went outside just in time as there were some boys hanging out in the alley doing whatever they do in the alley that late at night. Charlie went over to them and asked nicely if any of them had some jumper cables they could use and if they would be so kind as to give the two brothers a jump.

They pulled their car up to the brothers and popped the

hood, placing the red and black clippers on the terminal, and tried it, but it didn't start at first. They let it charge for a little while and on the third try the vehicle that was falling apart turned over. "She's alive," Jeff, the youngest brother screamed out into the dark Mexican night.

Charlie and the brothers hopped in and started cruising the streets drinking beer and smoking cigarettes. The youngest brother was at the wheel and started to get a little irritated by his older brother who was giving him a hard time.

"It wasn't me who messed it all up back home and robbed that liquor store," Jeff said to his brother Byron. "If it wasn't for you, I would be back home right now instead of being in this shithole. I'd be getting some from my girlfriend right now instead of having to go to some titty bar that smells like piss."

"You're an easy mark Jeff, you don't know what you're saying," Byron said to his brother, attempting to calm him down. Jeff began to lose all control, yelling incoherent obscenities shaded in his brother's direction. He started to lose all focus on his driving and ran a stoplight as Charlie protested the move from the backseat.

They were immediately pulled over for the blatant running of a stop sign in the middle of the night. There were three cops who got out of the car and Charlie could feel a world of trouble walking towards them as they made their way to the vehicle.

"Let me see your license," the oldest and scariest officer asked Jeff.

"I don't have one," he responded back defeatedly.

The three officers talked amongst themselves for a minute, trying to come up with a way to best extort them.

"Where is the marijuana? We smell the marijuana," the officer told Jeff, who immediately turned to the back and pointed at Charlie.

One of the younger cops told him to shut up after he ratted Charlie out and he couldn't help but laugh at the situation. Jeff pulled out the hash pen Charlie had handed them when they first got into the car and the three cops smiled at each other when he did that, knowing they would get something out of this deal, even if it was just the hash pen.

"You three can come with us to the jail now or pay us $500 dollars," they said to Jeff, knowing he would freak out the most by the looks of him.

It worked.

"What the hell are we going to do, Byron? We don't have that kind of cash," Jeff said.

Charlie asked the cops if he could get out of the car and talk to them, which they let him do. When he got out he reached his hand out and shook their hands. He apologized in Spanish for Jeff running the stop sign and informed them where they were headed and that it wouldn't happen again.

They told him to take the two brothers to the nearest ATM and to have them empty out their accounts if they didn't want to die in a Mexican jail.

"And they will die in there," the bossman said to Charlie. Going back to the car, the brothers were in a state of complete shock. After telling them what the police wanted from them, they informed Charlie they didn't have a penny to their names and they couldn't go to jail. Their mother would have to come down and get them out if they went to jail.

"Well, you need to go back there and tell them that," Charlie said. "I don't want them to try and get me once they figure out you guys have nothing to give them."

"Well it was your hash pen," Jeff said to him.

"And you didn't have to give it to them or say that we had one," Charlie told him matter of factly.

It was becoming apparently clear to Charlie he would end up paying for this one way or another and he accepted the fact. It was the only way out of this situation. So he went to the police, waiting patiently in their vehicle for their payday, and informed them they would go to the nearest ATM and get the brothers to take out anything they had in their accounts, which he told them was almost zero. After that they would have to go to the hotel Charlie was staying at in order to get some more money, he told them.

"How much do you want?" Charlie asked them again.

"We need at least $500 dollars, or you will spend the rest of your night in jail," the sergeant told him.

"I can give you $100 dollars," Charlie responded.

"That's not enough. You need to give at least $250 dollars to us for your crimes senor," the sergeant said with his jaw muscles contorting.

Charlie looked at him with complete despair, exasperated by the time of night and the heat.

"Look I just met these two jokers," he told them. "I have no idea who or what they are. I was just looking to get a ride home before that idiot decided to run a stop sign. If you have to take those two to jail and take my $100, I will understand."

"It's a package deal," the sergeant said to him. "You were all together, so you either go free together or you pay for everyone."

"Will you take $200?" Charlie asked.

"Si," he said as they quickly arranged how they would make the cash transfer. Walking back to the car, Charlie again realized they had taken his hash pen and that he was out of things to smoke.

"Do one of you have a cigarette you would bum a pobrecito?"

They smiled and handed him the hash pen before he went back to the brothers' car and got in, cursing the poor driving habits that led to the altercation.

They slowly drove to Charlie's hotel, stopping at every stop sign properly and courteously without mistake. They started to laugh it off and Charlie sternly warned them the police would just have him pay the bribe and then would pull them over down the road when they knew the brothers had absolutely nothing left.

"It was their style and that's when they really had you and you started to need to pray to your lucky angels or you were stuck in a hell of a jamb there might be no getting out of," Charlie warned them.

When they pulled into the parking lot, the security guards knew exactly what was going on as they laughed to themselves in the sweet delight of the little predicament. The police made the two brothers wait with them as a ransom and protectant from a run.

Charlie walked to his room and collected the money he'd stashed from himself as a precaution against overspending in a book he had brought.

Looking at the bills in his hand, he contemplated giving them a good old fashioned stiff. He was too tired to put that kind of energy into the situation, so he walked the long walk back to the hotel lobby where the police were ready to rid themselves of them and get their easily earned bribe.

They were out of there the second they had the money in hand and Charlie told the brothers they were welcome to leave the car parked and come get it in the morning, so they wouldn't get busted again by the same cops. They looked at each other, eyes wide open and heavy breaths protruding from their bodies.

"Let's get out of here Jeff," Byron said as they disappeared faster than the police.

Looking around and suddenly finding himself alone, Charlie decided to take another stroll considering this had been an eventful but piss and vinegar-soaked birthday. He walked with somber grace through the moonlight, characters scuttling in the shadows of the street, staring with wild mad eyes at his every move, waiting for the moment when he was the most vulnerable.

The convenience store offered the main source of light in the night, drawing Charlie out of the darkness and into the comfort of what looked like an American gas station. All the comforts of home-rolled out for him in the middle of the night in a Mexican alley. Charlie doubted even Donald Trump could have imagined walking like that around and smiling at people who disdained him because of the administration's current policy towards Mexico and of course all the name-calling.

The police who bribed Charlie lingered in the gas station, getting coffee just before the sun came up. Charlie made sure he bought them all a round of coffee and drank some with them in the parking lot.

"What do you think the biggest problem is right now between Mexico and the U.S.?" he asked them.

"The main problem is the gringos come down here looking for drugs, booze, and women," he told him. "That's all they want to do. To come to my country and get as fucked up as possible and puke all over everything. It's not us who are the criminals and bad guys, but people have to survive and they feed the gringos who want all that shit. It's the reason why I bribe the shit out of you people, so you will stay the hell out of my country."

They all laughed after he said this as if it was something amusing, but there was absolute truth to the statement and an air of general hurt.

When Charlie left the next day, he thought long and hard about what the Sergeant had told him on the drive home through a desert snowstorm.

The final battle of San Juan (for Charlie)

Charlie got back to Monticello on New Year's Eve. There were only a few hours left in 2018, a year that had its ups and downs just as every year, but this was the year Charlie had been pushed to his bounds as a father and man. He tried to muster the strength within him to go out and celebrate the end of the year properly but collapsed due to sheer exhaustion. He fell asleep in his clothes and awoke at midnight to the sound of fireworks exploding through the membranes of the quiet night.

"I hope 2019 is better than this year," he said to himself, turning on his side to go back to sleep.

He planned to immerse himself in his work over the coming months and that's exactly what he did. He took a vow on the drive back from Mexico he would change his ways and get exactly what he wanted from there on out in one of those moments of self-realization and clarity. He was going to get his family back. Then, he would have them join him there in the desert he was beginning to love so much. If he wanted it badly enough and worked hard enough to get it, surely nothing could stand in his way of achieving true happiness except for himself, he thought.

It was late January when he met Mary, the girl who set in motion so many things in Charlie's life and her own. Charlie was sitting in his usual spot at the speakeasy he frequented nightly, drinking away his pain and humanity one giant watered down beer at a time. She walked in, dark and beautiful, wearing cowboy boots and a magnetic smile. They both locked eyes on each other.

Charlie caught himself wanting her immediately but felt the conflict within his own heart. He loved Aubrey but still hadn't accepted the fact the relationship was over. For him, he still held hope everything would somehow magically work out, but the reality was he was lonely now. He'd been fighting alone so long now he'd forgotten what it felt like to be touched or looked at with a smile.

It felt good to have this beautiful girl look at him.

They naturally gravitated toward each other, Charlie breaking the ice and buying her the most expensive drink in the bar. She wouldn't take a drink of his absinthe and instead preferred a premium whiskey that Ken had cached behind the bar for a special occasion such as someone like Charlie wanting to impress a girl he'd just met.

"Cheers," Charlie said to her, clinking glasses together exuberantly. "To new friends, Mary. I think we're going to get along."

A few nights later, after exchanging numbers and several texts from the night they met, Charlie and Mary consummated their relationship. It was something Charlie felt extremely guilty for, but he thought of it as an eventuality and believed if Aubrey truly loved him, she wouldn't make things so hard for him in his life. That's what he told himself.

They spent their nights together, staying up until the sun showed itself to them, hiking into the desert canyons, exploring the beauty surrounding their forbidden relationship. She'd lived her entire life in the canyonlands and knew the land like she knew the people that lived there.

"They don't like you very much, Charlie," she told him. "They all think you are a shrill for Patagonia and you're here to try and pressure the locals to restore the monument."

"What do you think?" he asked. "Do you think I'm a shrill sent here to make your worst nightmare of restoring Bears Ears a reality?"

"I think you are lost and don't know where you are," she said to him. "It's ok, we've all been lost before. You'll find your way eventually after taking a few wrong turns."

"You think I got lost and took the wrong turn to get here?"

"I think you would be better suited for Moab," she told him. "There's nothing you can do about it, Charlie. This is the way it is here. They will reject you and make you leave. They don't want to change here. They don't want to change anywhere unless they're forced to. You're about two years too early, Charlie."

"I'm always too early or too late," he said. "There's nothing I can do about that. I get sent to these places I think for a reason. I try to show these communities there's a different way. They can accept people into the community and things can change, but they usually run me off and then it starts to change, gradually."

Charlie liked to think things changed gradually over time instead of all at once. He believed that because he heard a professor once say the universe was created gradually, and that nothing happens immediately. He tried to live that way but often found himself in immediate change. This situation was no different and he started to live a dual life.

There was the father in him who wanted his family that was slipping away. He tried to talk to Aubrey, but she would ignore him. He figured she was probably busy doing the same thing as he was, trying to find some kind of comfort.

Then there was the human in him that desired to be loved and appreciated. He knew Aubrey didn't appreciate the work he was doing. She didn't understand why Charlie wanted to delve so deep into local politics of a place like Utah. He would try to explain to her it was all leading to something. He tried to tell her there would be an opportunity of a lifetime coming along as a result of the hard work and determination.

She didn't care what he was doing. To Aubrey, the only thing that mattered was she had enough and that Joyce had a roof over his head and adequate means. None of the political stuff Charlie poked around in the styx mattered to her. It made her angry Charlie cared about it so much. She could care less what he wrote or what movement he was a part of, or who he was helping. She wanted him to care about his family more than he cared about his career.

Charlie dug in deep, aided by Mary and her local wisdom. He went about his life and was happy with what he was doing. He told Aubrey about Mary. She didn't care all that much, that's how she acted when Charlie told her.

She knew all too well he had already left her in spirit and it was just a matter of time before he told her he'd found somebody else. She was devastated and wanted to reconcile with him, but was unwilling to do anything other than try to convince him that the best interest would be to quit and come back to her and Joyce.

Charlie wanted no part of going to Wyoming to live and do an ordinary job to appease Aubrey. Wyoming to him was 30 years behind in their political ideology. He'd tried for years to do what he loved there with no luck. He would end up being a carpenter working for $15 an hour, cursing life. He found so much satisfaction and joy out of his work as a newspaperman that he couldn't imagine living without doing what he loved. He'd already gone without what he loved by not seeing Joyce. It was his everything to be able to wake up and do what he loved, which was working with local government and the community. He wouldn't let anyone take that from him and he dreaded the thought of giving up everything he'd worked for to have his family. There was no shame in it for him. For Aubrey, she resented the fact Charlie loved his work and openly hoped he failed in his endeavors and was forced to come back home to live a normal life.

After all, she was the one who had to give up her youth to have Charlie's son. Why shouldn't he be forced to make sacrifices, she thought.

Mary showed Charlie the Anasazi ruins, exploring the areas the Bureau of Land Management managed now. They walked through those crumbling ancient cities, gazing at the spiral petroglyphs Charlie frequently saw in Indian Creek and throughout the Canyonlands.

"This is what we don't want people to overrun," Mary said, pointing to a piece of pottery someone had found and set on a rock. "If they all come here and pick up a piece of pottery, before long there won't be any pottery."

"I hear that Mary, but lots of people around here tell me their family would put together entire pieces of pottery and keep them."

"My grandmother spent her entire life reconstructing a single piece of pottery," Mary said. "She managed to put it together completely except for one piece. She always searched for that one piece. I guess it was that one missing piece we all have in our lives."

"I feel like there's more than one piece missing for me," he said, looking at Mary in her natural habitat. She was free and uninhibited, something Charlie longed to be. "For every new piece I find, one goes missing."

"You know you could stay here, Charlie?" she said. "You would have to tone it down and just play the game. Don't be a player or an activist in it, just enjoy your time and the land. Don't get too caught up in it. This place is going to change. It already has. What you have to decide is if it's enough for you, or if you're like all the others who come here and trash it, taking little pieces of it with you to someplace else."

"I could spend a lifetime here and still not know it," he said to her. "There's so much in the Canyonlands to know and learn. It makes life an adventure to try and understand what these ancient people knew."

They hiked around Comb Wash and found more pottery shards and flint collections spilling over in mounds on the ground. Ruins dotted the landscape, springing up in disintegrated stacks of stone. Mary showed Charlie how to look for arrowheads in the wash and near the banks of dried river beds, telling him about artifacts she'd found in the past. Charlie had never found an arrowhead and questioned whether he would keep it if he found it. His old self would have put it in his pocket and never thought twice about it, but now he wasn't sure he could. He knew it didn't belong to him, even if he spotted it and the arrowhead had been waiting patiently hundreds of years to get discovered by Charlie.

They spotted what Charlie called a "rock castle" on top of a nearby hill. Later, Charlie learned the specific location they were at, something once called "scrotum rock" or more recently and politically correct, "walnut knob."

There were no trespassing signs prominently marking the rock face hill they climbed towards the notable geographical feature towering over Comb Wash. There were no signs indicating they were on Bureau of Land Management land, but Charlie was not deterred by the obvious signage meant to keep tourists away from sacred sites that had not been protected or thoroughly studied.

Like most things in Bears Ears National Monument, there were zero signs or maps showing what existed in the monument. There you were on your own as the explorer.

"Why do you think there's no sign even saying you're in a monument, Mary," he asked, trying to catch his breath up the steep slope. "I've never been to a national monument that didn't have a sign telling people where they are, or what was there."

"The monument has no formal infrastructure," she told him. "The locals don't want this to be a monument, Charlie. How do you not understand that by now?"

They looked out over Comb Wash, resting for a minute to perpetuate their conversation and enjoy the sunshine coming down on their winter faces. Charlie wished his son was with him and fought back the horses racing through his mind, trying to be in the moment, undaunted by the pain of the past.

"How could you not want to protect this and share it, Mary?" he said. "There's nothing in the world like this. I know you don't agree, but I have to be on the side that believes these places can be protected and shared."

"We don't want to share it, Charlie," she said looking out at the crystalline blue sky presiding over them. "We want to truly protect this place and keep it as it is. We don't want to change, Charlie, but it is changing. It's going to take some time, you know?"

He smiled and continued walking to the knob, looking at Mary, thankful for her presence and femininity that made him feel his own heart beat again. His time there was coming to an end and he would be helpless to stop that. He began to get that itchy feeling in his soul he wasn't supposed to be there anymore, that he had, just like so many times in his life, gotten lost and ended up in a place he wasn't welcome to be in. It wasn't home, only temporary.

They reached the magnificent rock feature, finding giant sections of rock that had through wind and water, split off and fell to the ground. They immediately spotted the largest pieces of pottery shards Charlie had seen in his limited time in the Canyonlands. They were vibrantly decorated, shattered in time after they were left in the ruins with no signs of why they were abandoned so abruptly.

When they went within the rock structure, there was a large panel of petroglyphs. There was a main image of a circle with what appeared to be a tree, approached on all sides by elk, deer and men riding horses. A separate group of petroglyphs depicted a snake, bird, cross like figure with a circle, and what Charlie thought was a turtle.

"This had to be a sacrifice spot," Mary said, looking at a slab altar at the base of the main petroglyph panel. "They say the Anasazi ate the warriors they captured in battle."

They stayed there for an hour, finding another panel of petroglyphs on the top of the knob. They found all kinds of shards, some from the same piece of pottery. They couldn't help themselves and collected dozens of them, placing them all together on the slab altar.

"They also say that if you wake the spirits of these places, or take something that doesn't belong to you, a great tragedy will befall you," she said to him. "I really want to keep this piece, Charlie. It has the most beautiful design I have ever seen on a shard."

"You can't take these things, Mary," he said laughing. "Then you will be just like the tourists they hate here, but rely on, just like everywhere else."

She reluctantly placed the piece with the other shards on the rock slab, putting on display the things they found, something that was most likely a federal crime. They both found comfort in the fact they didn't keep anything.

"We don't hate the tourists, Charlie," she said. "We just don't like the liberals that try to colonize our little communities from Colorado, or California. If you look around, you'll see a sticker on the back of everyone's car that says no monument. The locals just want their sovereignty to do with the land what they want. We don't want the BLM to tell us where we can and can't go. That's what we're fighting against here. We didn't like when Obama came in and designated this place a national monument without even listening to us. Trump listened to Orin Hatch and our local leaders and gave us the ability to do with the land what we want."

"Didn't they try to drill on the monument, Mary?" he asked.

"Look around you, Charlie. Do you think they could get a drilling rig up here? You're the one who the BLM played as their little fool to their true goals. They give you a little scrap, a news release about an area they are going to drill in or are looking at drilling in, but they have no intention of drilling there. They bait people like you to distract where they are going to put the well."

"I know they do that," he said. "They say one thing, but actually mean another. This isn't my first rodeo. That's why I do this job. It puts me in a position where I matter to the community and to myself. If I fail to keep people accountable, then I've failed the community."

"Then why do you champion these two Navajo commissioners?" she asked. "Those two guys need to be held accountable for all the things they've stolen from us. Grayeyes isn't even from Utah. He knows it, we know it, but nothing will be done about it. You're on the wrong side of this one, Charlie."

"We'll have to see about that," he said smiling and looking into Mary's blue eyes. "I have to go with what I feel is right here and I feel them trying to contest a legal election is just foolish. This lawsuit to strip him of his election victory is against the American democratic process. Nobody cares about the process anymore or what it means. It's all this Trump style of politics nowadays I feel like this is just about race and nothing else. He is a Navajo and they are white Mormons. It's been the same thing here playing itself out for well over a hundred years."

"Don't try to talk to me about race, Charlie," she said sharply. "I've been called every name you can imagine by my own boyfriends. That's what I like about you, I don't think you would do that to me. You see me for what I am, even if I disagree with you on the monument."

The reality was not many people actually moved to San Juan County and stayed. She wanted so badly to be able to have a future with Charlie, despite his situation with his son and Aubrey, which she listened to Charlie talk about way too much. She hadn't been around educated men like Charlie in her life. She knew nearly everyone in the county over her life there. She wanted to leave the place, but also felt conflicted about leaving the land she loved and knew.

She knew he would leave that place and ultimately her.

That didn't matter to her. She was happy at the moment and loved sharing her thoughts with someone who listened to her without judging her for her beliefs. That's how she felt and that is sometimes what is most important to people, even over the truth.

Charlie discovered his boss was ending his role as the editor because he was fired himself from the nonprofit he created. The publisher told him the paper was for sale and Charlie tried to leverage the new commissioners to give him a contract to go to the bank with, but the more he tried, the more he encountered resistance.

One morning Charlie went to work to put the paper together. It was unusually quiet and cold, with not many people moving around the town. He worked off the hangover from the night before with multiple coffees, piecing together the weekly publication.

"Charlie, I would like to talk to you if you have a minute," Phil said to him solemnly.

Charlie knew what was coming by the tone in Phil's voice. He had been trying to make the impossible happen and acquire the newspaper through sheer will and it had probably got back to Phil by now how Charlie was trying to acquire the paper. The two new commissioners agreed to explore the possibility of making a contract with Charlie in principle to handle their Economic Development Board advertising and outreach for a year. It was a longshot, but it was the only tangible way Charlie could purchase the newspaper, after getting turned down by the bank, and his family and his friends. His only hope to purchase the paper was through a direct contract with the county that would cover the entire cost of the sale. Then he would have to deliver on the contract for the year, something he probably couldn't do either.

"I've been hearing more things, Charlie," he said.

Soon after the conversation ensued, Charlie was without a job, crudely and hastily forced to pack his possessions. He was without the vocation his identity was built around. The things in his office were of little concession, the largest item being a giant reflective mural of a pack of wolves, which was jammed into the back seat of his car in a sort of disgust and disbelief.

I've come way too far at this point to just give up, he told himself. And with that, Charlie went about starting a spite publication to rival Phil's paper. It would be free of course and launched off of social media. The Grayeyes trial was that week and Charlie recounted his experience in a rogue article he published on February 7th, 2019.

The title of the article was: 'It's not about race, but the law...or so they claim.'

It read—

"A paralyzing January morning wind sweeps through the town of Monticello, Utah on what is unfolding as a modern American tragedy. It's a tragedy that is once again repeating itself as the courthouse in the small town is filled to capacity with citizens and witnesses amassed in both the courtroom and lobby. The parking lot is completely filled with cars parking down the connecting road 100 yards down the line.

San Juan County 7th District Court Judge Don Torgerson issued two orders in the civil trial prior to its start, requiring witnesses in the case to be called one at a time from the lobby room to testify on the witness stand. Many of the witnesses are there to give conflicting testimony from one another, but nonetheless, they sit next to each other in the lobby patiently awaiting their turns as they talk of things that have nothing to do with the case of Kelly Laws, a Republican County Commissioner candidate who lost the recent November election to Democrat Willie Grayeyes 973-814.

The second order issued by Torgerson required all media to get a judge's order 24 hours prior to the start of the hearing in order to cover the proceeding with a camera and electronic recording equipment. I arrive just after the proceedings began around 9:05 a.m. Upon talking with the court clerk, I found that no members of the media had filled out the required paperwork to cover the hearing in the professional and legal manner.

The day before I had been unceremoniously fired from the San Juan Record by Publisher Phil Boyle for three things that were "pissing him off." He got through the first one before the conversation took an angry twist and the middle-aged one-armed man resorted to shouting, "you dumb son of a bitch," while waving his arm around and kicking the closed office door open, sending my papers festooned across the wall in windfall. I had attempted to try and purchase the 104-year-old paper from Boyle, who had been the owner for the previous 24 years and the negotiation process had reached a dead end that day and I was delirious with his, "responsibility to protect the local viewpoints," which equates to withholding information like the Laws recording or outright writing the County was 5 million in the red over the past two years. He prefers to massage the facts in his home county.

I was going to the Grayeyes hearing more out of interest and professional involvement in the case over the course of the election and the filing of the civil suit. Laws had filed a contest to Grayeyes victory in the November election, bringing into question the Navajo activist's Utah residency. In August, Federal Judge David Nuffer ruled that the San Juan County Clerk's Office and it's Clerk, Juan Nielson had backdated a voter complaint form questioning Grayeyes residency, thus violating his civil rights. Nuffer placed Grayeyes back on the ballot and the voters of San Juan County, despite the question of his residency as a citizen of Utah, voted him into office as the District 2 County Commissioner.

Laws filed a contest to the election victory on Dec. 28, 2018, at 11:55 p.m. as he said at a community town hall meeting announcing the civil suit on Jan. 2 at the Hideout Community Center. Laws said many special things at the meeting, one of which I recall him openly saying that he would be named commissioner and that this case was entering uncharted territory. Several times during the course of that meeting, Laws foolishly took aim at the media for their "bias" or "fake news." I was the only media member at that meeting and he repeatedly looked at me while making these asinine claims. Commissioner Adam Bruce was present at the meeting the day after New Years Day and Laws and others kept trying to get him to weigh in on the possible civil suit, but he is too wise a politician and man to fall for that and he did add that he thought the redistricting of the county was especially damaging to him because he would only be able to serve a two-year term, compared to the two newly elected Democrats who would get to serve four year terms. Bruce also brought forth the fact that the redistricting of the county in 2018 was based off of a 2010 census that did not accurately depict who was living in some of those regions today. He also pointed out that it might be necessary to redistrict the county based on the new upcoming census when it is completed.

Laws did try to play off the race card and say this is not about race, but rather about the law and Grayeyes not being a resident of the state. I recorded the entire meeting and sent it to Grayeyes and National Public Radio immediately after the meeting, something Boyle later tried to reprimand me for. I still have a copy of the "Spartacus" meeting in its entirety, something that amuses me everytime I listen to it.

The courtroom was so full on Jan. 22 that I was not permitted to enter the courtroom as it was completely full. A bailiff went around the lobby handing out DMV type tickets with numbers on it, a sort of lottery system for those wanting to get a seat when it became available. I had a blue #4 ticket and decided to call George Briva and see if I could get the forms to attempt to gain access as a media correspondent. It was amazing to me that nobody was there to officially photo document the proceedings, or legally record arguments. George sent me the forms and I filled them out, giving the email I created at the San Juan Record to combat Boyle's grossly outdated system. I put "SJR" as the media outlet, as I created the Indian Creek Observer later that night.

Judge Torgerson signed the document and I was permitted

to enter the jury box as the only media correspondent who could legally photo document, record, or video the proceedings. Many recorded the proceedings illegally, but I wanted to play it right in this situation. I set up eagerly awaiting the second half of the eight hour hearing after the recess. I ran into Kelly Laws at the convenience store during the lunch break and jokingly said to a friend within his ear shot to never trust the "enemy of the people" and "fake news." The look on that man's face was priceless. He entered the courtroom with his attorney Peter Stirba, who Laws championed during the Jan. 2 Spartacus meeting as nearly unbeatable and that he would never take a case he couldn't win.

Stirba started after the break by calling his witnesses, trying to create a case out of Grayeyes not having a Utah driver's license and a residence Grayeyes bought in the 1980's in Page Arizona. Stirba failed to grasp through his conventional terms the very geographical location of Navajo Mountain and the Navajo way of life, which is very different from his own. Repeatedly Stirba tried to confine the Navajo way of life there into a neat little package that can be defined by the white man's way of life, or a piece of plastic or utility bill.

One by one, Stirba made the case for Willie Grayeyes with his fundamental lack of understanding of a different culture altogether from his. It was hard for me to see him try to define a Navajo man's way of life through the lense of his white privilege and system that took everything from their people not that long ago. His argument was fundamentally mucked from the beginning, and it was even more hilarious to watch his self conviction and assurance in his arguments, which carried with it zero actual proof of anything. At one point he lost his pen as it launched out of his hands when he began to become frustrated. By the end of the hearing, Stirba was being overturned on nearly all of his objections and had visibly already lost the case.

Mr. Boos, who represented Grayeyes along with two others that day, made every Navajo witness introduce themselves in the traditional Navajo way. This he later told me was done for the conscious reason. The traditional Navajo introduction includes the place you are from, your clan, and where you live currently or work. Boos masterfully revealed traditional Navajo culture throughout the hearing, revealing many aspect of the Navajo culture that maybe were unknown to Judge Torgerson, such as how property disputes are handled, probate processes, grazing leases, and the space each Navajo is given in time and space with the burial of their umbilical cord, which forever sows one to the land in Navajo tradition.

Mr. Boos also asked Kelly Laws when he took the stand where he got his news. Laws again looked at me and said that the news is bias and that he relies on the townspeople for his news. Boos specified the question and asked Laws where he got the information for court cases related to Grayeyes and San Juan County Clerk John David Nielson. Laws again said he got his news from the townspeople in this regard. Laws also said on the stand that he never said at the "Spartacus meeting" that he would be named commissioner. It was painful to watch, but a la mode of Trump's America.

The "Burden of Proof" was on Laws' camp the entire hearing, and there was no proof presented that absolutely proved his claim that Willie Grayeyes lives in Arizona and is not eligible to be a San Juan County Utah Commissioner. All that is needed for a county commissioner to be eligible to hold that office is one consecutive year of residency. Stirba was going back as far as the 1980's in some of the history and at one point brought up the death of Grayeyes wife in the late 80's, none of which was pertinent or bore the burden of proof. Stirba's case rested on a piece of plastic, an Arizona driver's licence which Grayeyes had. It was revealed that almost everyone who lives in Piute Mesa, or Navajo Mountain had Arizona license plates and driver's licenses on account of the distance to the nearest Utah DMV, which is four hours away compared to the DMV located an hour away from Navajo Mountain in Arizona.

Next Stirba brought a sheriff's deputy who conducted an investigation on the Navajo Nation into Grayeyes residency, which the San Juan County Sheriff's Department has no authority or jurisdiction to do investigations there. Torgerson did not accept the investigation findings in his court due to this reason.

Ultimately Stirba and Laws civil case didn't pan out as Laws described it would to the people at the Spartacus meeting on Jan. 2 where he promised he would be named commissioner if Grayeyes were stripped of his office as commissioner. Judge Torgerson said at the end of the Jan. 22 hearing that he would render a decision on Jan. 28, but did not end up releasing the decision until 5 p.m. on Jan. 29, which quite predictably ruled Grayeyes is a San Juan County resident, and ordered reasonable attorneys costs to be paid to him for the pragmatic Laws civil suit.

As I told many before the case and after, Laws would be better serving the people of San Juan County by accepting his defeat in November and the fact a Federal Judge and a District Judge have now ruled Grayeyes is a resident and won the election and is the sitting commissioner in District 2 for the next four years. He would help the county by putting his residency concerns into another campaign and going about things in the good ol' fashioned Democratic way of winning elections. Because after all, the voters of San Juan County knew the score and voted Grayeyes in over Laws regardless.

Laws and Stirba have filed an appeal to the ruling by Torgerson and thus have ensured that there will be continued division and obstruction to the new commissioners ability to focus on the monumental issues within the county, such as a emaciated general fund due to foolish lawsuits based on a crusaders mentality. Even if they were to eventually win, which they will not, they are serving as an example of the tragedy that has been playing out now for some time and will continue to play on until the light bulb comes on. But don't forget, this is about the law, not race, or at least that's what they claim. Where is Mitt Romney when you need him to say he's from Utah with a smile?"

* * * * * * * * * * * * * * * * *

Charlie had succeeded in completely burning any bridges he may have made in San Juan County. He knew it wasn't his home, they wouldn't have him. It was their home they had stolen from someone else who had in turn stolen it from someone else. The locals didn't want anybody else living there except themselves. He would have to continually fight an uphill battle to be able to stay there. It was worth it at the time he was there to fight all the battles. It was just the part in his life where this is what was happening to him. He was fighting on every front and fighting to get the truth out. He was fighting to see his son and he was fighting to make it in this world. The world could care less.

Charlie loved what he did with every inch of his soul. He felt a purpose in creating the newspapers. It was a certain amount of normalcy that was generated when he was putting together the paper. It calmed him and gave him a peace that nothing else short of being with his son gave him. He felt an artistic release come with taking photos, going to government meetings, and writing the articles. His work was the only constant that hadn't been taken from him.

"Why is it that they get to control the narrative and own all the things," he asked Mary. "I have more talent than Phil will ever have in his life and he can't stand that. He went to Harvard and has all the credentials, but just never had it. He has the money, the family, and the backing but is lacking the balls."

Mary laughed at the last part.

"It doesn't matter, Charlie," she said. "He has what he has and he will always have it. He won't sell to you and none of the locals even want you to have the paper. They think you're a liberal that works for the democrats. They will never think any different about you. You're also not in their church and to them that is everything."

"I've been talking with a newspaper in Hawaii," he said. "It's on the island of Kauai and I think there's probably a pretty good shot I get the job. I've talked with the editor there before and the timing just never worked out. If I got it, would you come with me?"

Mary stared at him and then smiled, contemplating her ticket out of the canyonlands.

"Being with you in Hawaii would be paradise," she responded. "I could just imagine us there on the beach-loving life. It seems like a fantasy."

A few weeks later, they were saying their goodbyes to each other in an airport parking lot. Another love that could have been, but never lasted. One in a series of endless possibilities that never come to be.

Mary cried and begged Charlie not to get on the plane and go to Hawaii after they spent a final day together hiking Arches National Park and walking under the Delicate Arch. He knew he had to get on that plane and his future awaited him on the other side of the flight. She knew she could never leave the canyon-lands. This was most likely the last time they would ever see each other.

She hated him for that and always would.

A first Hawaiian

Charlie landed around 10:30 p.m. Hawaiian time to find no nightlife on the island to speak of. That's what first occurred to him despite the fact a dry hurricane just rocked the island. When he got to the gates of the hotel after a long taxi ride in the rain, the urge to collapse onto the ground and take a dirt nap became real. The manager who received him was sleeping on the couch when he arrived and didn't awaken easily.

The manager was trying to slip into the comforts of the end of the night and Charlie was impeding the progress of that. It was something that made them at odds no matter what after that fact. Charlie went straight to his room and collapsed with all his clothes on only to wake up a few hours later still drunk and confused to where he was and why. He made his way out into the early morning Hawaiian sunrise and tried to coherently understand the place he had come to and exactly why he had made such a journey in the first place.

He left the confines of the hotel and wandered on the walking trail, where there were trees snapped in half like toothpicks from the dry hurricane which passed over the island without conjuring up a full-blown hurricane. He was a week earlier than he was supposed to be there for work, something that never happens on aloha time.

The residents jogged, walked, and biked along the path in the early morning hours, all of them around retirement age for the most part from Charlie's first observations. Moths that looked like hummingbirds fed from the nectar of the flowers that aligned the side of the path. The path meandered along the beachline and Charlie kept a watchful eye looking for monk seals or whales that might be on the horizon. Before he knew it, a distance of several miles had been walked as he called those closest to him and those that had driven him to go to this island in the first place. None of them answered and it started to dawn on him he was alone on an island in the middle of the Pacific Ocean without knowing a soul.

There was a convenience store near the road, a little distance off the bike path humming with activity by this time in the morning. Inside of the small gas station, Charlie found his first copy of the Garden Island newspaper and bought it, ready to scan over it several times to dissect the finer nuances that made it what it was.

"The key was to look for the small details," he told the clerk half deliriously. "The things that made it what it was and gave it its character and reputation."

The paper's reputation was something of a dispute to what he had heard thus far in the game. Some said the paper lacked certain objectivity as it related to the publication giving a voice to the local Hawaiians and their thoughts on issues like the Coco Palms, where Elvis filmed "Blue Aloha" that was now a skeleton ruin, leftover from the mercy of Hurricane Iniki in 1992. Since that time, it had been reclaimed by the land, and not long before his arrival, it had been claimed by a group of Hawaiians who said it was the land their ancestors were buried on and deeded to them through perpetuity.

It was a topic that had created lots of debate in the past year as new developers had taken on the project to breathe life back into the ruins. The first thing they did was to come in with bulldozers and take out all of the encampments that were on the property when they got the contract for it.

The locals who were living there and attempting to survive off the land in a simpler way of life immediately sued. A court battle followed in which the judge gave a favorable ruling to the two developers, Tyler and Chad. These two had some kind of backing in St. George, Utah, and vowed to restore the property to its former luster.

The other topic at hand at the moment was Mark Zuckerberg, who had moved to the island a few years earlier and was now creating a doomsday complex, or at least that is what some people were calling the thing.

He built a wall surrounding the property the locals now shit and piss on with constant frequency. They were upset he'd come to their good island like a colonizer and set up something that was what they could never do. They looked at him as what he was, a rich genius dork who was nothing without his money.

An auction was scheduled for a few weeks where he was attempting to buy some buffer properties surrounding the 700 acres his complex sat on. He had undisturbed beach access, which in Hawaii there is a state law beach access must be granted to all.

You add in the fact the Hawaiians believed their kuleana lands there were passed down in perpetuity from their ancestors, you had the recipe for animosity and the feeling they were being colonized again. It was something the locals there took very personally, especially the families that had to go up against Zuckerberg in an auction for the land they owned.

The calls were returned to Charlie after a short while. First, they came from Aubrey. The one who had driven him to the furthest lengths of the earth over the past five years and left him without anything to show for all his self described hard work and dedication. At least that's how he saw it.

She knew Charlie was going away for good this time, even though he would be back eventually.

It was not an easy pill to swallow for her considering they had once had a life together that was promising. Then the gears of reality started to make the wheels fall off and change as it is always doing. There was hope they could work it out somehow, but with every passing day, the prospect of having resolution became a pipe dream.

They had not talked for at least ten days before Charlie left for Hawaii. It was a common theme between them — that is to emotionally abandon or completely abandon all together only to offer nothing as a respite at a later date.

Aubrey would not let Charlie have any time with his son outside of her motherly clutches and had kept him away from Joyce going on seven months. It dug at Charlie like a dagger turning him inside and out and there was no relief from the pain other than living and living fast. That was the plan, to get over the pain they had inflicted on each other and to heal in some way over the coals of tropical living. Charlie's goal was to have her eventually come to the island if she would. At least that was his goal and it had never worked out to this point, so there was the prospect of diminishing hope and the feeling of missing out constantly on his mind.

There was a feeling inside coming to Hawaii was the biggest mistake he could make, considering she would in no way visit him or make an attempt to have his son come and visit. It didn't matter if Charlie was there to do a job or anything like that, that was what they would use against him later in the custody battle that dragged on for two years. This wasn't their first go-around at this game and Charlie knew it would most likely end in the worst possible fashion, but for now, he was abroad and was positive of the fact he would do everything in his power to make a go of this and make it work out for the best.

He called his son and showed him some of the sites, which he looked at with intention, but was unable to comprehend what was going on. After they talked for some time and Charlie felt a little better, they said their goodbyes, and Charlie wished he was there with him, or he was there with him.

It would be a long time before Charlie would get to hold him in his arms and that thought alone brought an uneasy feeling. He fought against it as hard as humanly possible. The easiest thing to do was to pretend the problem didn't exist, to drown it away. The more it consumed his mind, the more it destroyed his life.
He hated her but loved her. Loved her, but hated her. Needed her, but disdained her. Wanted to forget her, but couldn't get her out of his mind.

Forgetting her would not be an easy task for Charlie, but he deemed it a necessary task for him to move on with life and start to heal from the long toxic relationship they had endured rather than enjoyed.

"It was sad, but every attempt had been made to do the right thing," he told himself going to bed that first night on the island. "For years she refused to try and create a better life for her family. After more and more time passed by and the same thing happened over and over with no change whatsoever, the insanity began to work its way into his mind. For the longest time, he thought it was him and that he could somehow fix the problem by doing something different or attempting to make Aubrey happy in some way.

He got good jobs and houses, moved them to communities that offered a better prospect of financial success, and did everything in his power to make the woman happy. It only made it worse and the fights would start, sometimes lasting for weeks at a time. There was nothing he could do but accept it was ending. All that was in the past now and didn't really matter, but he couldn't let it go. He would sit for hours on the beach those first days trying to come to terms with the things that were and the things that had now become a part of the past.

Joyce didn't understand what was happening, although in his young mind he just wondered what had changed. He couldn't understand why his dad was mad when he talked to him, he just wanted to talk to his dad. He would dream at night about his mother and father getting along and playing with him. He wanted them to get along.

His mom was always sad, and that made Joyce sad. He didn't know what it meant to be sad yet, but he was feeling that emotion. Sometimes he would see her smile, it was when there was a new guy that would sleep in her room at night. Joyce liked the man, he was nice to him and would give him toys sometimes. The guy and his mom would go to the racetracks sometimes on Fridays. There were monster trucks and cars that went fast. He loved the red car, it reminded him of his favorite Disney movie character.

The "millionaire" and the "houseless"

Charlie's job was not ready for him when he arrived early. There were drug tests and protocols to be done before he could work a day. Being early is something you dare not do while residing in aloha time and the Hawaiian archipelago. You will often be punished for being early there. People will be suspicious of anyone who is early and or on time in the Hawaiian islands. It's out of the ordinary and will make you stand out like a sore thumb or the loudest Kauai rooster in the morning.

There were roosters everywhere and anywhere you went.

The island was overrun with feral hens and roosters which crowded the beaches and were in every imaginable location. From the famed Waimea Canyon, which Mark Twain called the Grand Canyon of the Pacific, to the deadly Queens Bath which claimed the lives of dozens of people in the decade preceding Charlie's arrival. The Kauai rooster was a force to be reckoned with and Charlie was told by locals they were descendants of a great Polynesian fighting fowl that crossbred with Hawaiian chickens. Later he read in the Los Angeles Times that many scientists believed they were just birds that they, "can be traced to the aftermath of 1992's Hurricane Iniki, which devastated Kauai, destroying many chicken farms, from which the birds literally flew the coop."

Early on in his time there, Charlie was spending it trying to figure out how he was going to make it on the island, thinking it over at a popular waterfall site. There were hundreds of chickens running around, feeding on things the tourists threw at them when out of the corner of his eye he saw a car pull up and an occupant ran out and grabbed a fierce-looking rooster, covering the cock with a coat. The kidnapped fowl didn't protest much as the man threw him in his car and sped away.

Charlie was no stranger to the ways of cockfighting, having spent time in the Dominican Republic one winter when he was trying to run away from his life, or rather another woman. He would frequent the local cockfighting arenas there and marvel at the Dominican national sport (besides soccer) and all the cash that was thrown around betting on fowl fighting to the death.

He knew there was cockfighting on the island, but despite all his attempts, he could not find where it was taking place. The main problem he was encountering with his short amount of time on the island was the problem with housing. There was an over demand for housing and not enough houses for everyone there and he had only just arrived fresh off the boat. He stayed at one of the two hostels on the island when he arrived but was far too old for that, but far too poor to stay at a hotel until he found a vehicle and a place to stay. He was certainly fresh off the boat and only had the two bags he carried with him.

Before leaving Monticello by way of tar and feathering, Charlie searched the usual channels for strange deals and arrangements. It was one of Charlie's main strengths in the world to find odd things and circumstances and somehow hack a living out of it. He'd come across an ad for someone looking for a security guard to look over vehicles near the airport. It sounded like something that was up his alley and Charlie sent an email using only proper English and complete sentences. He knew it wasn't going to be easy there and he even faced it he may have an incredibly hard time starting there while he got his legs under him.

Charlie got a call back from the person who posted the ad looking for security and after talking to the man named Joel Fryer, he deduced the guy was looking for someone to stay in a van and make sure that nobody broke into them.

Joel Fryer owned a local rental car agency. Its basic concept was to rent the island going tourist something that didn't stick out to the locals and meth heads as something to rob and or hit with your truck. He also knew if he made the rentals cheap enough and the vehicle ran down enough, there were profit margins and a consumer base to be exploited.

He'd got the idea after moving to the island as a young adventuring Joel Fryer, freshly graduated from high school in Maui. He took his graduation money and moved to the Garden Isle and bought a junker island car to get him around. The man who he bought it from didn't tell young Joel there was a problem with the engine. It blew after Joel drove it around for a few days and the guy refused to pay him back the money for the car. Fryer took him to small claims court and won some money out of the deal and then used that money to buy two island junkers.

He would rent them out to his friends when they came to visit him on the island and soon had a full-blown car rental agency, later adding a tire shop and many other sketchy business affairs to his fold over the years.

Joel Fryer leased a small lot from the Federal Aviation Administration near the Lihue International Airport where he stored banged up cars he bought for a tremendous discount. He would then collect the insurance money on the cars and get them repaired, selling them for a profit. The process took time, but Mr. Fryer was a man willing to wait any amount of time to squeeze a profit out of nothing.

After squeezing enough profits out of island cars and everything he could, Mr. Fryer became a rich man, a millionaire. But if you asked him, he was just getting by.

There were a plethora of millionaires who'd sauntered their way to Kauai somehow or another. There were many shades of them.

You have the standard inheritor that will tell you they are an important this or that, but in reality, they are just a product of their father's money and will never surpass their father in anything. Rather, they find they are the best at holding an air of superiority to just about anyone and they are better at spending money and taking money from others than most.

There is the tycoon, who through hard work and staying alive long enough here, has made it where most fall short and others just come because they can't hack it on the mainland. He and she, through a combination of sheer force, have made their presence known to the world and continue to be felt through a combination of influence and business dealings.

There is the billionaire. Like Mark Zuckerberg and Elon Musk, who frequented the island and in Mark's case, lived on Kauai. Tesla had just built a 52 megawatt "Tesla Powerpack" and a 13-megawatt solar farm on island.

The average person on Kauai overpaid for their energy through an electric co-op that was the only on island. Their board of directors all made over a quarter-million dollars. They comprised your form of millionaire of the local and corrupt who'd slithered their way along long enough to sell out and laugh their way to the bank.

There was also your standard vacationer that had money through whatever they did back home and came here to blow off steam or look at the pretty sunsets and usually to get married. The hotels they stayed in were considered awesome on paper, but in reality, were crumbling to pieces after being blasted by the salt heavy air and unending sunshine. They were all desperately in need of renovation and in some cases, they just needed to be torn down and rebuilt from the ground up.

The locals worked the hospitality hotspots on island as a means to an end. For them, it was a way to make it and survive on island. They loathed the visitors, but at the same time, needed them. The visitors in turn didn't care about how the locals felt because they had just paid a bunch of money to come there and they could do whatever they wanted because they damn well paid good and plenty for it.

That was the essence of the place. A daily back and forth between the two entities. The locals were the side taking the brunt of the price to pay with all the different forms of millionaires surrounding them, driving up their property tax and forcing them to get two and three jobs to pay their property taxes. The houses they owned were family houses, with three generations living in them. Many of the families were leaving the island and moving to the mainland because it was becoming impossible to keep up with the costs of the exploding rent and basic necessities.

Then there was the mass population of homeless living on the island, or as some tried to call them and be politically correct, "houseless." They would live in encampments such as the one nearby where Fryer had his lot at the airport where his cars were constantly under the threat of being plundered by the houseless these politicians spoke of.

That was all just a part of the game. It was food for the lions and the only solution was more money. After a week on the island and nowhere to live after being ousted at the hostel, the stage was set for Charlie to work for Mr. Fryer fixing his problem at the airport lot.

Charlie met Fryer at a local Chinese restaurant near the newspaper office. Charlie arrived before Fryer and ordered some lunch. The plan was for Fryer to show Charlie around and see if it was something he wanted to do. That's how Charlie understood the plan.

For Mr. Fryer, he didn't want to disclose too much information before meeting Charlie in person. It was nothing against Charlie or anything like that, it was the fact he had gone through literally thousands of emails, calls, and meetups. He'd learned through experience the meet and greet was the way to go about verifying if the person could handle the task at hand. There had been many who'd come before Charlie at this job for Mr. Fryer and there would be many after.

Charlie's predecessor ended his stay at the airport lot in the van by calling the police in a frenzy. He was too afraid to come outside the van when they arrived. He reported during the call they were trying to kill him and if he stepped outside the van he would be hacked to pieces by their machetes.

When the police got him to come out of the van, the man was delusional and screaming they were banging on the van and saying they were going to kill him. He told them they were on all sides with their machetes squealing like pigs, screaming they would spill the haole's blood that night and drink it.

Mr. Fryer didn't mention any of that information to Charlie before taking him to the lot after having some lunch at the Chinese place. He hadn't been there in some time and was happy Charlie had called him to meet up.

Mr. Fryer had a companion, Luke the dog. Luke went with

Mr. Fryer everywhere he went, even the office of the rental agency. Luke had his own spot complete with a dog bowl and bed. He would sometimes piss on the floor when he got too excited by customers who would pet him. Mr. Fyer would promptly clean it up with a paper towel and apologize for Luke's excitement.

"This is Charlie, Luke," Fryer said to his dog as they got into the car.

Luke smelled over the passenger Charlie, who looked back at the dog with little interest. Charlie wasn't fond of dogs.

Mr. Fryer told Charlie the genesis story of Island Rental Cars, the business he'd started in his early 20s. Of course, he embellished the facts and reiterated to Charlie he was, "not a gearhead or anything like that."

Fryer started his rental car business after buying a used car from a used car salesman on island. After driving it for a week, the car broke down on the young Mr. Fryer, forcing him to go back to the man who had sold it to him and demand a refund.

"The car worked fine when you drove it out of here," the salesman said to Fryer. "It's your burden to take care of the car after you drive it off the lot."

Fryer left the used car lot after arguing for reimbursement unsuccessfully. Seeking retribution after not being satisfied with the answer he was given about his now useless island car, he went to the courthouse and filed a small claims case against the car salesman.

He sought reimbursement in the amount of purchase ($3,400) and most importantly, compensation for his time and effort spent on the vehicle that was what he termed a lemon.

The salesman claimed it was an act of user error and the engine had blown due to Mr. Fryer's actions and not of the fact he knowingly sold the car with a faulty engine.

The court sided with Mr. Fryer and awarded him the full amount he had purchased the vehicle for in addition to $2,000 for his time and effort. With the money, he decided he needed to buy two island cars in case one of them blew up so he could still be mobile.

With the extra car, he would rent it out to friends and colleagues who needed a car when they visited the island.

"That's when the light bulb went off and I knew there was something there, Charlie," he said. "Then it just kind of started like most things here I guess. There was a need and it just kind of grew into what it is today."

Charlie pretended he was interested in what he was saying and that it held significance. Charlie didn't care in the least. He didn't view Fryer's standing in the world as something to be impressed with. He thought he was still on the mainland.

They came to the lot near the airport with all the pristine convertible rental cars and off-road vehicles the major rental car agencies owned. There were thousands of vehicles there amid their afternoon shuffle as men and women drove them in and out of the gated lot with a constant frequency. It was an endless shuffle of moving this car to the front and returning this car to the back.

Joel Fryer drove past the first gated entrance and into the second one where they drove to the back of the lot where the jungle and shoreline met. There on the edge of the treeline rested around 100 of Joel Fryer's vehicles. They were stored there awaiting their day to be fixed and sold for a profit.

"I want to build a bus here that is a converted living space," Fryer laid out to Charlie. "It would have solar panels and a bathroom with an attachable shower. It would also need to have a perimeter tripwire and a spotlight. I'm going to look for an old one at an auction this month. Although, I'm sure I will have to make all the modifications once I find it. That's just another phase of this project."

What Charlie saw at the lot and what Joel Fryer saw were two completely different things.

Fryer saw it as something with potential that could make an endless profit if controlled right. He believed the only problem standing between him and that goal was the stubborn meth heads and their constant looting and plundering of his vehicles. He figured if he could fix the problem at hand, there would be nothing stopping him from letting his busted-up cars someday be restored and sold for a generous profit.

Charlie saw it as a means to an end. It was someplace he could ride it out until getting a few paychecks under his belt and a place to stay. He saw it as a pathway to landing on the island and studying it until he could make decisive actions that would allow him to survive without having to run home. He also saw the danger in the situation. There was a distinct possibility he could be killed out there in the middle of the night.

Fryer took him around the lot and showed him firsthand what had been happening there at night and probably in the day. There were signs of extremely fresh plundering, possibly from the night before.

"Yup, they were here recently," Fryer said to Charlie, gritting his teeth. "Dang it. I can't stand these guys. Ah, look at that."

Windows were smashed and batteries were excavated with hoods propped open by force. Giant colorful Hawaiian Garden Spiders made their homes in the open trunks and doors of cars. This was a graveyard of vehicles that would never get fixed, but it was the principle of the matter Charlie guessed that kept the wheel turning.

The winter rain made a soft feeling come over both of them as they explored the lot and assessed the damage. They left after it started to come down with more intensity, driving to the rental car agency Mr. Fryer was so proud of. When they arrived, Charlie filled out a little form that gave Mr. Fryer his basic information such as credit card number (Charlie gave him a debit card number that was expired), address (Charlie did not have one), and emergency contact (Charlie put his mother's number who would not talk to him). When the form filing was done, Charlie and Fryer took a stroll among the rental cars. Fryer picked the worst of his entire fleet that consisted of over 150 vehicles to give Charlie.

It was your basic island car. Over two decades old with tread bare tires you could see the metal thread poking through. It had seen plenty of use over the years in Fryer's fleet of cars that ranged from the moderately used to the all-out island car junker that barely ran, to the car he just loaned to Charlie.

Many times they didn't run, requiring Fryer to run around

the island and rescue stranded tourists he rented unreliable cars to. His day conjured many things, but mostly it consisted of fixing an endless array of problems that never ceased to arise. Luke helped him get through the stressful days.

When they tried to fire up the old car to make sure it ran, it refused to turn over. They tried it a few more times with no luck. Fryer quickly diagnosed the problem as being a faulty battery, having seen the problem thousands of times during his business tenure. Fryer pondered it over for a minute out loud.

"Hmmm, what to do," he said to himself pausing for ten seconds. "Ok."

Fryer decided it best to go buy a battery and replace the faulty one to get it running so Charlie could look over the lot. The quick math in his head told him it was a worthwhile investment.

On the way to purchase the new battery, Fryer got a call. His phone was constantly ringing and he hardly answered it knowing full well that it would be some trouble he would have to take care of immediately. He and Charlie quickly changed their course, headed on a rescue mission of a customer who had broken down.

They stopped by the rental car agency and Fryer instructed Charlie to get in one of the cars at the front of the shop and to, "follow me, but drive carefully because the tags on your car are expired."

When they arrived at a cockroach infested motel in what Charlie had ascertained was the "city" on the island, Lihue, they found another vehicle in need of a new battery. The customers were not happy and made it known while Fryer and Charlie looked over the car for any obvious reasons why it was not working.

After several attempts to turn it over and realizing it wasn't going to happen, Fryer gave the customers the car Charlie had followed him in. The customers, in a hurry to explore the island for one last night before they had to catch a flight back to the mainland, were doomed to lose an hour to battery trouble. They were a husband and wife, presumably from the midwest given their lack of tan despite being on a tropical island and the University of Wisconsin sweaters they both wore.

"How did you enjoy the island?" Charlie asked them as they

were about to leave.

"It's amazing and we don't want to go home," the wife said to him with a smile that told him she was lying.

"It would have been better if we had a car that ran and didn't break down on our last day," the husband said passive-aggressively to his wife so Fryer could hear it loud and clear.

Fryer said nothing in response and continued to look for a way to get the inoperable vehicle to start. After the husband and wife left on their inevitable journey back to the midwest in the car Charlie had followed him in, Fryer pulled out the tow rope and hooked it up to the running car. Charlie got on the ground and hooked it to the beached car. Fryer didn't want to get his Hawaiian shirt dirty.

Charlie rolled in the Hawaiian dirt, happy to be of use, linking the two vehicles together with the tow rope. It felt good to do something.

"Do you know how to keep the tension tight?" Fryer asked Charlie, who in turn nodded his head.

Fryer started the car and pulled the line tight as Charlie eased on the brakes to increase the tension. The two vehicles careened onto the street and eventually the highway, making their way back to Fryer's shop as the sun started to hide behind jagged mountains, running behind the ocean.

They got there and unloaded the impotent car next to the junker. Fryer felt safe letting Charlie use it for no money and work trade. They later returned with two fresh batteries and replaced them with the use of artificial light to guide their hasty work.

There was a struggle in the fixing as they had to modify a few things to make the battery fit to the car Charlie was going to use.

Eventually, both the cars started and ran without labour or dying. Fryer and Charlie shook hands and agreed it was a job well done that day and he would look over Mr. Fryer's problem at the airport lot.

"You better not let her run too long," Fryer said. "She is running on fumes and the gas station is about three miles from here."

Charlie thanked him reverently and hopped into the silver car he named Independence. The car rode about as good as it looked and sounded, crackling every so often with a fierce roar letting Charlie know to slow her down.

He rolled into the gas station as it ran out of gas. He coasted his way up to the pump and breathed a sigh of relief. Charlie found gas was the most precious commodity on the island as he poured his precious funds down the gas tank.

"I've got to get some damn gas or I'll be walking," Charlie told himself, cognizant of the fact he would run out of funds before he got paid his first check at the newspaper. He was going to hit zero. His work promised him they'd refund the cost of an airplane ticket and travel expenditures.

Now that he had secured primitive transportation and lodging, he could rest easy knowing he had a start to build with. He drove quietly through the night, thinking about what his son had done that day. He wanted to call home and talk to his young family and say he was sorry and everything was going to be alright, but he knew better.

He pulled into the pitch blackness that encompassed the airport lot at night. He entered the area that was marked off as Fryer's lot and turned off the engine, which crackled with the change.

Charlie sat there in silence, wondering what the hell he was doing here.

"I should be at home raising my kid and working at a pizza place if that's what it takes," he thought to himself. "Paradise isn't worth the price of the ticket if you can't share it with the ones you love."

The thought of Aubrey infected his mind like a Hawaiian centipede sting, coursing through his veins slowly. Charlie tried to numb the feeling so he didn't have to feel the pain.

He'd been in a position like this once before in the past. The only difference was this time there was more on the line and he was older than he used to be then. His best friend predicted this would happen to him long ago. It had been years since Charlie had talked to The Sir. He hadn't seen him since the time they said their goodbyes in the Dominican Republic five years prior.

He called his old friend and gave him the breakdown of what was happening in Hawaii, overselling the facts and embellishing on how good he had it. He left out the part about how he was almost paralyzed with poverty and grief about not being able to see his son.

It didn't take long for Charlie to convince The Sir to get on a plane and come find out for himself what was happening there.

"It sounds like this Fryer character is a good friend to have," The Sir said to him. "I wonder what else he is hiding? I bet he has some irons in the fire."

"I don't know what he has going on, but this island is unlike anything else," he said. "You have to come and see this place. It is like the Dominican only better and in America. You remember all the trouble we used to get in there? It could be just like old times all over again."

"I remember," The Sir responded. "I remember how you left me on that desert island all alone with nothing but Dominicans to keep me company while you ran to Europe, thinking you were destined to marry some Austrian. That was one of the best times of my life, minus the almost dying part. I'm in brother, I'll be there soon."

The Sir was the kind of man to be where he said he was going to be. It was one of the only things you could count on him for. That and to have a handle of vodka at all times. He would ceremoniously kill it throughout the course of however long it took him to do so. Sometimes it would be fast, and other times it would be slow. It depended on his mood for the day and availability of funds.

The Dominican Republic

Charlie and his two friends, The Sir and Luna waited at the gate of their plane bound for Punta Cana, Dominican Republic.

They'd just been living in Ocean Beach, California together for a few weeks before getting kicked out of the hostel. It was over a fight Luna started with two gentlemen who had successfully secured the women he wanted.

When he came across the two gentlemen making out with the girls on the steps of the hostel, a few unkind words were spoken and the instigation that was needed to spark the fire ignited a barrage of fists, most of which Luna landed. He thrashed the poor two gentlemen who licked their wounds in the arms of their waiting new lovers after the fight was all said and done.

In the morning, the owner of the hostel fired Charlie after reviewing the security video from the night before.

The footage clearly showed Charlie stopping Luna after he threw the first punches successfully into the jaws of both gentlemen. The two gentlemen then, in turn, punched Luna despite Charlie's intervention and the fight was on. Charlie didn't get involved at that point and went about letting Luna resolve the situation.

"It's clear what the problem is here," the owner said resoundingly to Charlie. "Alcohol."

Charlie didn't argue with the owner, who had weeks earlier tried to sell the establishment to him. Charlie had served as the manager for the summer and believed the offer was to get the city of San Diego off his back for the numerous violations of city ordinances he was perpetually committing.

Instead of arguing with a pro, Charlie politely asked for his check and thanked the man for allowing him to have the experiences he did.

He informed Charlie he and his two friends needed to check out of the hostel immediately that morning. Also telling him to not come back for some time. He warned young Charlie against the dangers of drinking as he was prone to doing, telling him he'd wasted a golden opportunity there. Then he said he could pick up his check in the morning when it was ready.

They shook hands and went about their separate ways. Charlie knew the old man was in the wrong, but he didn't want to be the bearer of bad news and tell him so.

The old man knew that Charlie was on the path to becoming a drunk traveler, the worst form of traveler in his opinion. He then went and had a drink in his office to calm his nerves.

"I wish that son of a bitch the best of luck, he needs it," the owner said to himself in a cheers.

"It's better this way," Charlie thought to himself. "In the long run, this wasn't home for me. It was a great experience, something I will remember for the rest of my life, but it was just a party. You can't make a home out of that, it has to be something more. I could see living here forever, but it would be like living on borrowed land. It wouldn't feel real to me. "

This is what Charlie told himself, but deep down he knew that it was a chapter ending in his life never to be re-lived. He knew it was a fleeting moment in time that would never be recaptured or recreated. He would always think of the time he spent as a time pursuing the lesser evils of managing a hostel in San Diego, California. His first summer in California would be etched in his mind for as long as he lived, one of those times in a person's life where they did what they wanted because they wanted to experience the world for themselves. The liberation of youth.

It was a time in his life he would also forget the small details of, but remember vague generalities like the ocean breeze coming in at night or the smell of the rotting kelp washing up on the beach in the morning. He would remember the feeling of being young and alive with the possibility of the world at his fingertips and nothing was holding him from making his destiny except himself.

He would miss the endless hordes of young European tourists trying to live the California lifestyle if not for a short amount of time to tell their friends and families back home in the distant future that they were able to do it, live that cinematic American dreamscape that is the California of the mind, but in reality, is a third world country where the rent is too high for the putrid small living space you're unlucky enough to inhabit and have to fight to the death for. And just outside that living space is the trash-strewn across the landscape without care.

He went into his room where his two friends waited out their hangovers, trying to figure just what it was that they had done the night before.

"We're out," he told them. "They want us off the property within the hour. There's nothing I can do about it this time boys. The old man couldn't be talked out of it no matter how hard I tried. He told me there is an alcohol problem afoot and that I need to leave because he just can't have that kind of drunkenness. He thinks it's bad for business even though that is the business here."

"There's a guy here that overdosed on heroin the other day and he's worried about our drinking?" The Sir said. "They found him passed out in his puke which was almost completely the Ramen noodles he had been mowing down. The noodles were soaked in tequila. And still, the old man let him stay even though the ambulance had to come get him. They must hate you for something else, Charlie."

Luna looked around, his eyes beading with the sweat beginning to trickle slowly down his shaved slick forehead.

"I'm going to get the tickets now," Luna said to the two of them. "Are you coming with me?"

Charlie and The Sir looked at each other for a moment, silent. Their eyes locked in a knowing of what they were in for if they decided to go down that path and follow Luna. They simultaneously began to shake their heads in a confirmation they were going to the island where Christopher Columbus had landed mistakenly thinking he was somewhere else. It was the place where Christopher followed his dream to the island of Hispaniola where the Dominicans to this day claim he is buried despite the Spanish confirming Columbus is buried in Seville, Spain.

Charlie knew nothing of the history of the Dominican Republic or what it had to offer, he knew the weather was nearly perfect and the water, as he was told by Luna, was as warm as a bathtub. The icing on the cake was Luna told them he had a place for them to stay free of charge until they could, "find a place or something."

It sounded too good to be true to Charlie but he took the plunge nonetheless. He listed the car he'd driven out from Colorado to California for sale, hoping it would be enough to get him there.

The car was spray painted black with green trim. Charlie bought it for $600 and added new things like tires, a battery, windshield wipers, alternator and got it tuned up before making the journey out to California to start his new life.

He'd found he needed to start a new life from his old new life before it all got too familiar.

"This can't be as good as it gets," he told The Sir. "There has to be a better way out there somewhere. California can't be the best there is on the face of this earth. There's too many people and too much pollution. You can cut the crazy with a knife in the air when the sun starts to go down."

"I don't know about that, Charlie." he said to him. "There's a reason California gets so much play and attention. It's a one of a kind—kind of thing. There's nothing but imitation out there and only one California."

The Sir knew what he was talking about when it came to California. He was born and raised there and narrowly escaped there a handful of times, including two Colorado stints in the federal penitentiary. California always got him back in the end and it had again after he served his time for past sins, setting the record straight in trial that Charlie had nothing to do with any shooting nearly claiming a life and a pair of cowboy's testicles. The Sir only did six months for that incident.

Luna knew nothing of Charlie and The Sir's past and he didn't care much on account of being from the Dominican Republic. He'd seen his fair share in his life and knew the two gringos would meet their match of craziness on the island.

Charlie got several quick bidders for his car, but still didn't have much time to get rid of it. Haste was made and he sold the car to the first person who looked at it. He was lucky to get anything out of the Isuzu at all as the transmission started to go out as Charlie was driving the car to the guy who bought it.

"I don't know," he told Charlie looking over the car. "It looks like it needs a lot of work."

"It's running and has all these new things," Charlie told the man. "Look, how about you give me five hundred cash and we call it good?"

The man hesitated before responding, "you got a deal, but barely."

They shook hands and Charlie got the cash, calling a cab to take the three to a hotel near the airport. They loaded all their belongings and Charlie arranged for a ride to the hostel the next morning to retrieve his last paycheck.

Luna bought the tickets with his credit card and Charlie and The Sir paid their part of the shares. They packed their bags and got rid of all the unnecessary things for the journey, which amounted to a few trash bags full. One of the items deemed unnecessary was a bag full of blue mushrooms which The Sir had.

"Here, Charlie," he said. "Eat as many of these as you can, we need to get rid of them. I'm probably not taking these on the plane with me."

"I'm not eating any of those things tonight," Charlie said. "You've got a ton of them. What the hell are you going to do with them?"

"I thought we would eat as many as we could tonight and then eat the rest of them before we got on the plane," The Sir responded. "It's guaranteed to be a splendid special kind of time."

"It would be a nightmare," Charlie blurted out. "There's no way I'm eating any of those things before I get on the plane. I would freak out and they would immediately arrest me and send me to the nearest institution."

"You'd be fine," The Sir said. "It's the best way to fly, but if you're not interested then you can give it to someone at the hostel when you go. There's bound to be somebody who could put these babies to good use. Just give it to the person who you feel could use it the most."

With that, it was decided what to do with the unnecessary items and the trio spent the rest of the evening ordering take out and getting beer at the nearby gas station.

In the morning Charlie went to retrieve his paycheck, leaving the mushrooms on the sidewalk near a trash bin. He figured somebody would find them, most likely a street person who would then turn around and sell it on the boardwalk. He liked to think it would help somebody, but it was found by a young man who sold them and used the money to buy some heroin, later overdosing from his habit nearly a year after.

Charlie said his final goodbyes to the morning staff and gifted his heavy books he could not take on the plane to the hostel.

One of his former colleagues asked him what had happened and he responded, "I'm not sure."

When he got back to the hotel, they took a cab to the airport, taking off and landing in Miami where they waited for several hours before catching another plane which landed in Punta Cana, Dominican Republic. From there they took a cab to Luna's house which was an hour away from the airport.

Charlie and The Sir silently looked out on the Dominican landscape which was, "crudely erected and made in a haste," as The Sir put it.

Charlie watched the townsfolk walk around with baskets on their head as the men whizzed around on their four-stroke motorcycles, or hung around in groups on the street corner.

They were exhausted and didn't know what to expect. Luna told the two, "I haven't been home in two years or seen my wife since then. She's waiting for us at her house. That's where we'll be staying."

They knew what that meant and it wouldn't be anything but a matter of time before she would turn on the likes of the two gringos staying in her house.

"She's Norweigan," Luna said. "She doesn't like gringos either. She hates them."

Luna brought along a new computer which he'd bought as a

peace offering to his wife Anja. It was meant to calm everything when approached by her husband whom she hadn't seen in two years and the two nameless gringos by his side who'd come there seeking debauchery and exploitation of the island.

The cab pulled up and Anja was there at the front of the house to greet her long lost husband. Her face was pale and devoid of the muscles necessary to formulate an expression of happiness that carried on it a perpetual look of displeasure.

Not having been told any of this before coming to the island, Charlie and The Sir were a bit taken back. It got even worse when Luna informed the two he was not allowed to drink in the presence of Anja.

"She thinks I don't drink anymore," Luna told them whispering while unloading luggage. "You can't say anything about what we did in California or about the drinking. I will drink with you guys when she's not around, but I have to be careful. I'm on thin ice anyway."

"What the hell, Luna," Charlie said, quieting himself when he saw Anja poke her head out the front door.

He kept his silence.

Luna showed him and The Sir their quarters, which was a single room with the main bed and a smaller one with a mosquito net. The Sir headed straight for the one with the mosquito net, instinctually knowing what lurked in the soon to be darkness.

When they settled in and unpacked a few of their things, Charlie and The Sir went on a walk to see their surroundings. Luna was busy explaining to his wife why he'd been gone for two years and why he had two strange gringos with him.

They were in the town of Cabarete, which is one of the best kitesurfing locations in the world. Walking the main strip they saw the lights on the beach of the clubs and the swaths of aggressive prostitutes coming to them to offer up their services.

They made their way to the nearest liquor store after passing dozens of motorcycle taxis who endlessly called out, "moto?"

"We're going to have to take hundreds of these rides while we're here," The Sir said, staring at the little four-stroke bikes. "Jamb up nice and tight and grab on to your friendly moto-taxi driver, the Dominican way."

"Do you know how to drive one of those things, Sir?"

"I know how to drive them, but choose not to out of fear of dying from my horrible motorcycle karma," he said.

Neither of them had the faintest idea of how to drive a four-stroke motorcycle the way that would be needed to navigate the island. The Sir had much more ability in that respect than Charlie who had never driven a motorcycle in his life. It was something that never interested him and he would rather walk given the circumstance as to avoid what he was beginning to notice as a common theme of the locals walking the street with a crutch and a missing leg.

They denied the services of at least two prostitutes on their search for a liquor store, something that didn't make The Sir all that uncomfortable, but made Charlie extremely out of his element. He would ball up as they approached him, giving the prostitutes the sense he was an easy target and could be easily had if they tried just a little bit.

"There's a pharmacia," Charlie blurted out. "I hoped they would be here like they have them in Mexico. There is no better friend to a gringo in these parts than that of a good pharmacist who understands the pain I am in. The pain is unbearable and there must be some remedy to relieve me of the suffering and sickness I endure on the daily."

They walked in, Charlie's eyes nearly bursting, looking at the Latin American candy store of pharmaceutical drugs before him. He looked at everything, not leaving one aspect of the store untouched from his examination.

He wanted it all. Even the trinkets and touristy stuff collecting dust.

The Sir talked with the pharmacist, who in turn recommended a cheap painkiller for his "back pain." He bought the entire box which had four sheets of 25 pills on each tinfoil sheet. They each took one and got a bottle of rum at the liquor store next to the pharmacia.

The ocean called off the boardwalk and they stumbled out into the darkness where the Caribbean stars made themselves known. They walked across a pack of wild dogs, which were everywhere, chasing a donkey down an alley.

"What the fuck are we doing here man?" Charlie said to The Sir, passing the bottle of rum. "We had it pretty good a week ago in California and now we are in the middle of a third world island nation that neither of us knows a single soul in outside Luna."

"It's worse, so it's better," The Sir said, taking a swig from the bottle.

The Sir was 34 at that time and Charlie was just turning 27 in a few weeks. They both had no clue what they were doing with their lives but didn't care to get all caught up in that. They both held a common belief most people were not living their lives but were just going through the motions of it all, missing out on the stuff that mattered. To them, nothing mattered anymore at that time in their lives than to get drunk by the beach and enjoy the time they had then as free men not enslaved to any notion or dollar, but to that of their own volition.

As the time passed, the two gringos became separated from the Dominican that had brought them there in the first place. Luna was trapped without any means of escape by Anja and he liked it that way. He had just brought the two along as a means to give Anja something to focus on and dislike more than himself.

One day, Luna informed them they both had to pay rent, spelling the end of the living situation that lasted two weeks. Charlie had met a British fellow who'd married a local nearly twice his age. He was a giant amongst men, standing 6' 5" with fire-red hair. He was a cook who came to the island much in the same fashion as Charlie and The Sir, but when he landed on tough times, he met a local girl who turned out to be the woman of his dreams. She helped him back on his feet and in turn, he promised to marry her, which he did without hesitation.

She was a nice girl named Isabella who took care of the chef from England with all the Dominican comforts she could offer, which was not very much, but it suited him just perfectly. To him, she held all he ever needed in life, unconditional love.

Charlie met Davey at a fruit stand after inquiring about a motorcycle he was selling and they quickly hit it off. He told Charlie he needed to be wary of Luna, that Dominicans were notorious for bringing gringos to their home country and extorting all they could out of them.

"If things don't work out with that guy, don't hesitate to give me a call, mate," Davey told Charlie. "My neighbor has an apartment for rent in the barrio if you need the place. It's cheap and clean."

Charlie took down his number and filed it away in his back pocket in case the offer was ever needed.

A few weeks later it was needed as Charlie, The Sir, and Luna had a falling out of sorts.

"You dirty gringos need to pay rent," Luna said to them.

"You're dirty," The Sir responded. "You're the Dominican who said he had a place to stay free of charge and is now singing a different tune. You think we would have come here if you didn't offer that?"

"I don't care what the offer was, it's changed," Luna said. "If there is one thing, it's that Anja does not like The Sir. She thinks he is dirty and an alcoholic. She is sober and refuses to be around anyone that drinks."

"What the hell, Luna," Charlie blurted out. "A few weeks ago you were drinking more than any of us and going on any date you could manage. Now you act like you're some kind of saint to impress Anja when you're dirty and you know it. We call that being a hypocrite where I'm from."

"I don't care," Luna responded. "I need you two to pay rent or leave, today."

And with that, Charlie approached the friendly gardener he'd come to know with while living there. He was from Haiti and kept trying to get Charlie to go on a trip with him there.

"Juan, do you think you could give me a ride to my friend's house?" he asked. "There have been some complications with Luna and we're no longer going to be staying here on account of these complications."

Juan agreed to give Charlie a ride and he quickly packed up his belongings in the giant duffle bag he'd traveled to the island with a few weeks before, throwing everything he owned into it and zipping it up. He loaded it carefully on his lap, balancing the weight symmetrically as to not tip the scales on the small four-stroke. Charlie didn't have a phone but knew where Davey King lived in the barrio.

He arrived at Davey's front doorstep uninvited with a giant duffle bag full of junk and was greeted as a friend by the jovial Brit who invited him inside as Isabella cooked them a humble meal and poured them Presidente beers.

"You were right about that Luna," Charlie said to Davey. "He is trying to get us to pay their entire rent. It was a setup."

"Don't feel bad man," Davey said. "You're not the first one who came to the island on a promise to live rent free. It's a paradise, but the scams go hand in hand with the beauty. That's why I speak Spanish and check everybody I do any deals with. They rip you off and never think twice. That's the Dominican way to some of them."

"Does your neighbor still have that place for rent?" Charlie asked him.

They went next door and Charlie rented out the roof of a two-story house from Davey's neighbor. It featured a veranda with an excellent view of the barrio, overlooking the street and the neighborhood store which was next door.

Charlie paid his new landlord $300 for three months and went to the little store next door and bought two liters of Presidente beer for him and Davey. They sat on the concrete blocks on the veranda that all the houses were constructed of. This particular house was not finished, like many of those in the country, and would get built brick by brick for decades until it was finally completed.

"Not a bad spot for three months," Charlie said. "It is a little weird the bedroom is a completely separate building and so is the bathroom."

"Let's go look at that bathroom," Davey said, walking to the door.

Davey opened the door and they both gazed at the new bathroom in astonishment.

"It looks brand new like they just built the thing," Charlie said to Davey. "The only thing missing is the toilet seat. I bet that will be hard to find here."

"Your bathroom is nicer than mine, Charlie," he responded. "Nobody uses a toilet seat anyway except for women. It keeps them from falling in."

They finished their beers before Davey took Charlie on the back of his motorcycle to retrieve The Sir, who was still in the room where he and Luna were arguing.

"Sir, let's get out of here," Charlie said. "Pack your things and hop on. I've got a surprise for you. Luna, we're out muchacho. It's been great romping the streets of Ocean Beach with you and gracias for your hospitality."

"Pinche gringos," Luna mumbled to himself as they walked out the door and all three of them jumped onto Davey's motorcycle, riding off into the sunset of the barrio.

For the next few weeks, the new trio of Davey, Charlie, and The Sir romped around the island with Davey keeping a safe distance from the two newcomers while they caused trouble.

The Sir and Charlie got to know every moto-taxi in town. They quickly grew a reputation as the only tourists ever seen who walked everywhere they went. And walk they did, making long voyages. The taxi drivers would drive by ten times in an hour, all of them honking and offering their services, hoping to be the ones who could dissuade the two legendary walking gringos from walking.

It never worked and the duo took pride in not being like everyone else and doing it their way. After some weeks passed, the moto drivers began to resent the pair. They would holler nasty things at them. Things Charlie and The Sir could never understand considering The Sir spoke no Spanish and Charlie spoke his American high school Spanish class Spanish that was incorrect. The dialect there was nothing like traditional Spain by the book Spanish he learned out of a textbook. The Dominican dialect was more of a blend of Creole, English, and colonial Spanish.

"It's not even a language," The Sir would say. "They don't speak a recognized language. That's why they all wear those shirts with upside-down crosses because everything is upside down here.

It's upside down because you're looking up at the cross from below the equator."

The Sir never attempted to speak the language and therefore managed to navigate much better than Charlie who refused to speak his native tongue to the locals. Instead, Charlie spoke a sort of broken Spanish that made him incomprehensible to most, except the tourists who were visiting from Spain.

This gave The Sir much more street credit with the moto taxis, who they found out were run by the syndicates. One night, The Sir went out without Charlie on the strip, coming across Luna along the way. They shook hands and buried the past as Luna was especially happy after managing to escape Anja for the night, free to drink and romp as he pleased without fear of repercussion. It was like the two were back in California for a night.

"La Pistola es en la casa," Luna would yell out after taking a shot with The Sir.

"El Senor," The Sir would respond, rolling his tongue as long as he could on the last syllable.

They made a night of it, painting the strip a special color red. Luna introduced The Sir to everybody he knew along the way, which was nearly everyone they came across considering Luna was born and raised there, although he claimed to be Spanish.

"I'm not black El Senor," Luna informed The Sir quite seriously. "I'm Spanish. I'm not like these Haitians that are so black you can only see their eyes at night."

"I don't care if you're black," Luna," The Sir answered. "It makes no difference to me whatsoever. I'm from Los Angeles. There they would call that racism and you'd get sued, senor."

The Sir was growing tired of Luna and was ready to call it a night on account of his funds running low. He said his goodbyes to Luna and respectfully shook his hand as to leave on good terms. When he walked out the door he saw a group of moto men. They recognized The Sir and knew they had him alone this time.

"Moto, moto, moto," they called to him. "You need moto?" The Sir didn't say yes or no, which was a sign of disrespect to them, but to him, it was perfectly normal. They began to follow him thinking he might have something of value on his person they could easily rob. They were mistaken, he had nothing.

The Sir, knowing this game all too well, reached in his pocket and clutched his pocket knife. He knew it was a small defense, but a defense nonetheless.

He pulled it out of his pocket and showed it to the three moto men following ten yards behind, taunting him. They laughed at this display and followed closely. The Sir, undeterred, continued with his same pace toward the barrio and the safety of home. When he entered the barrio with the three following him, continuing to taunt, every dog at every house erupted into barking. The progression of noise woke Charlie.

The Sir stood at the gate without a key, holding his pocket knife ready to give a stabbing or cutting to anyone who lunged at him. They began to make their move.

"There's a camera here you burros," Charlie yelled at them. "It can see all of your faces."

They looked at each other and instantly dispersed on their motos, cranking them up and driving off into the noise of barking dogs, drowning out their cries with the sound of their fleeing.

"What the hell happened?" Charlie asked The Sir, opening the gate for him.

The Sir said nothing as he walked to his bed and went to sleep, explaining the story the next morning over coffee. After that night, the duo never went out alone without a liter of beer in their hand so they could easily bash anyone to death in case they were overtaken at any given time.

They carried on like this for a few months until Charlie decided he'd had enough. He didn't tell The Sir, but he made arrangements to get off the island. He bought an airplane ticket to Brussels off Davey for a discount. Davey couldn't use the ticket because he had some financial troubles and could no longer afford to make the annual trip back home to the United Kingdom.

"El Senor, I have something to tell you," Charlie told his friend. "I'm out of here. I bought a ticket the other day and I'm headed to Europe. I'm going to go and see a nurse I met back in California from Austria. She told me to come to her estate and I've been thinking I'm going to take her up on the offer."

"I figured as much, Charlie," The Sir said to him. "The problem is it will never get any better than this. This is paradise. There's no better reality out there I promise you."

"There's got to be," Charlie informed The Sir. "This can't be as good as it gets. The beaches are white and the water is as warm as a bath, but this can't be it. There are better things out there. You can't make this place your home. You're a tourist here, the moto drivers will get you before it's all over."

"If you say so," The Sir said.

The next week Charlie arranged for a friend they made in Cabarete to give him a ride. It would be in the middle of the night the next town over to the nearest bus depot. It was the only route to catch the bus to Santo Domingo. From there he would catch his flight to Brussels and then make his way to Austria and be happy ever after forever. At least that was the plan.

On the final day in Cabarete, The Sir and Charlie celebrated like it was their last day on earth. They made a final round around town on foot, seeing all the spots they'd drank at over the past six months.

For Charlie, it was the end of a chapter of his life and the beginning of another. For his friend, it was the beginning of his time on a desert island alone, but undisturbed by the habits of Charlie. He would be free to enjoy paradise alone and not be forced to constantly listen to him wonder out loud if the grass is greener on the other side. He could sleep in and have his home in the barrio all to himself. He might even begin to teach English to the local kids so he could appear to be doing something of use to the community.

"I'm going to get the quintessential picture of me in the barrio surrounded by children, teaching them English, Charlie," The Sir would say to him while thinking about his future in the Dominican. "That would mean I made something of myself, there would be no denying it then. I could show it to people for the rest of my life."

Charlie purchased some charcoal roasted corn and a machete at the local hardware store, which he visited for the first time on his final day on the island, regretting he hadn't come earlier. The corn was for him and The Sir to eat after several Presidentes and the machete was a gift for the nurse he was to visit.

"She's going to hate that thing, Charlie. Maybe even kill you with it. Or worse."

"What could be worse than her killing me with it?" he asked.

"You don't want to find out, but I'm sure you could use your imagination," The Sir said nodding his head and slashing his throat with his finger. "She's going to go for your balls once she finds you sleeping with one of her friends or her sister."

"She doesn't have a sister, Sir," Charlie said, shaking his head.

"You know what I mean, Charlie. They all have a sister of some sort, even if it's one of those best friend deals."

Charlie asked nearly everyone they encountered that frantic day in the Caribbean if buying the machete was a good idea or tragic one. It was a clear consensus the gift was a terrible idea, so they bought a painting to go along with it.

They ran into one of their friends, a street artist named Leon who sold paintings along the roadside amongst a plethora of other things he sold. The painting Charlie bought from Leon to take to the Austrian nurse named Emma was a surrealistic knock-off of Salvador Dalí. Not too bad considering Leon had no formal education whatsoever and he painted to make extra money to feed his daughter. It was something to kept his mind off the harsh realities surrounding his daily existence.

Leon knew everyone in Cabarete, having grown up there and hustling a living off the streets. He was a renaissance man of the Dominican and nothing would ever slow him down. Leon had grown to like the pair of gringos. He thought they were funny and enjoyed their general good nature. He also didn't mind the fact they loved to drink Presidente beers and were very generous with them.

Leon decided, in honor of Charlie leaving the island, he would do something he wanted to do since the day he found the place. He wanted to take Charlie to the one place he hadn't been to in the barrio yet, so he could see what it was really like.

The place was named "Barrio Blanco." It was given the name by the syndicates for the product they sold there, cocaine. Leon didn't tell Charlie where he was taking him just to build up the suspense in his mind and to heighten the fear. He kept telling him to, "not say anything when we get there and to do whatever was asked of him."

When the sun went down, Leon told Charlie to get on the back of his motorcycle and again, "not to say anything." They rode a few blocks from the barrio Charlie and The Sir lived in.

Little did they know just down the street from where they called home was a drive through cocaine store, guarded by all the worst characters one could imagine. As they rode the motorcycle into the entrance of the dark labyrinth responsible for most of the bad things on the island, Leon killed the motorcycle and told Charlie to get off and walk. Leon began to walk the bike with him.

"Remember what I told you, Charlie," he said. "Just keep quiet and don't do anything, especially talk."

Charlie nodded his head in agreeance, walking behind Leon, keeping his head down despite the gazes from the group of men holding guns and smoking various things. They started to talk to Leon and he froze, putting up the kickstand to the motorcycle and leaving it where they stood.

The men all laughed and carried on talking amongst themselves in the shadows of the early night.

Charlie saw what looked like a small octagon building with windows where people stood in line. About five people were waiting patiently in line from what he could determine, most of them were white middle-aged men.

Charlie could hardly believe it was that easy and this had been here the whole time, serving day and night without his knowledge. He wondered if he would still be alive if he had known about this place when he first got there.

When it was their turn, Leon talked to the man and told Charlie to hand over the cash.

"How much?" Charlie asked.

"It's twenty dollars for a gram," he responded.

Charlie looked at the man and handed him a twenty-dollar

bill and a ten. When the man inside the hut handed him the gram and the ten-dollar bill back, Charlie insisted he kept it as a "tip." The look on his face told Charlie he was not pleased with the gift and he handed the white powder to Leon for keeping.

"They would love to set me up right now just before I leave, Leon," Charlie said to him. "If they find it on you they won't do a thing and let you keep it. You're a Dominican, they would almost be disappointed if you didn't have any on you and hold it against you."

The pair walked before the group of men in the shadows again and kept their heads down on their way to the parked bike. Leon got on and started his trusty steed, flipping it around before Charlie jumped on the back and they slowly drove out of Barrio Blanco with the lights turned off. Once they got far enough away from the men with the guns, Leon turned the lights back on and they drove as fast as they could in the opposite direction. They went to the local corner store and got some beer before heading back to The Sir and the apartment Charlie had rented in the barrio, which was soon to be The Sir's permanent home.

The three of them laughed and drank until the early morning. Leon was asleep on the floor snoring when The Sir looked at him and said to Charlie, "You see what you're leaving me to work with here? I'll be forced to work with Leon while you desert me on some desert island. It's ok, I'll be ok, don't worry."

"I wasn't worried," Charlie said, looking at Leon on the floor. "This won't be it. There will be other Caribbean adventures down the line. I'm sure of it."

"No there won't" The Sir responded. "You're going to go to Europe and get all euroed out and wear strange boots that won't be as cool as the boots you have on right now. Then you'll end up marrying that girl and she will trap you in Austria forever. Then there's going to be no way out for you sir, no way at all. And then she'll murder you with the machete you bought her because looking at Leon's painting drove her crazy."

"That sounds like a real possibility, Sir, but I'm afraid it's not going to end like that," he said laughing. "We'll be having a drink together at some strange bar in no time at all, I guarantee it."

And with that, Charlie woke up Leon, who was to drive him to the bus station the next town over, nearly 30 miles away. Charlie fixed his bike for him so it would make the journey without stranding them in the middle of the night. They didn't want to be at the mercy of the highway pirates who they prayed they would not encounter.

Charlie and The Sir said their goodbyes coldly and crudely. The Sir realized he would brave the island until he couldn't do it anymore. He would be forced to go back to the mainland and live like a normal person again, but that was in the future. To him, that was a fate worth avoiding at all costs, even if it meant living on summer sausage and crackers in paradise.

Leon drove through the night with no headlights to keep the pirates from seeing them and then killing them both for Charlie's luggage which contained almost nothing of value except a 1969 edition of the National Geographic which featured the moon landing and had a record, "Sounds of Space," still intact, inside the magazine.

When a light peaked over a faraway ridge, Leon would pull over into the bush and wait until it passed. After doing this several times, making considerable distance, the lights of the town revealed themselves through the night to their collective relief.

"We're going to make it without being brutally murdered," Charlie yelled to Leon and the night. "I'm going to miss you Cabarete. You were a hell of a place if I say so."

"The best," Leon said back.

They arrived in a sleeping town. Only the cats stirred at this hour, moving sporadically to the flickering lights. They had a parting beer which Charlie had ready for the occasion. He thanked Leon for getting him there safely and wished him the best with his art. He gave him a hundred dollar bill as a token of gratitude. Leon knew he would never see Charlie again and he was ok with that. Charlie thought he might one day see everybody again, so it didn't cross his mind this would be the last time he saw his Dominican friend.

Charlie drank another beer and took some oxyfuerte he had

bought at the pharmacia before leaving. He was dead tired as the bus pulled up and he boarded, keeping his luggage close at first and then using it as a pillow on the empty bus. Slowly, it began to fill as he faded off into a deep sleep before waking to the noise of everyone getting off at the last stop in the city of Santa Domingo at the airport.

Charlie got off the bus, blinded by the light of day. He was in a button-up shirt he'd been saving for the occasion, which he put on before the motorcycle ride. He looked terrible. It didn't matter much to him as he flagged down a cab and had it take him to his terminal where he continued to drink heavily before boarding the flight to Brussels. He looked at the atm and contemplated exchanging his money in pesos for euros, but decided against it.

"I'll be able to do it when I get there," he thought to himself, having a last drink before boarding. He took a few more oxyfuerte before the call for final boarding came and he hurried to his gate.

Not long after takeoff, he fell asleep for what seemed to him like days. He floated in the clouds alongside the airplane to Europe, headed on a European adventure. He had always dreamed of going there. He was going there and knew it in his dream.

When he woke up he was very pleased with the thought he was on his way to Europe for real. Nothing was stopping him now he thought to himself, all too confident in his natural ability to travel alone.

The most intense turbulence of his life hit a few minutes later in the middle of the night. Bags were coming out of the overhead compartments and the lights had turned off. Charlie looked at the faces of the people who were in absolute terror. One person got out of their seat as he fainted and others around him were puking. Charlie reached for his little travel bag and got a few oxyfuerte, choking them down without water. He started to drift off into his mind and before long all the other noises drowned out and he fell asleep peacefully in full chaos.

He enjoyed a traditional airplane Belgium breakfast consisting of coffee and delectable waffles in the morning. The crew was cheerful in the morning sun, speaking Flemish and smiling to all the stressed-out passengers. The plane landed at seven in the morning and Charlie was surprised to see the sun was still not up. He went through customs and had his passport stamped, gaining entrance into the country.

The first thing he did was to go to the ATM to get some European currency and another breakfast. He was surprised at first to find he couldn't withdraw money from his savings account. He tried on all the different ATM's in the airport before finally asking some of the employees running around what the problem was.

The people were rude and didn't have the time to talk to Charlie. He tried again and again, thinking he was maybe doing something wrong. To no avail as he found the same result each time, ending in him being unable to retrieve any money.

A man suggested he look downtown to the banks, which were due to open soon. To do that he would have to ride the train. The problem with this is that the train cost money, which Charlie did not have.

He knew what he was going to have to do. It didn't bother him to hop the train as much as the thought of being stranded in the airport with no way to figure out the problem that haunted him the most. The choice was clear and he hopped on the train with his backpack, duffle bag, and giant duffle bag.

Nobody checked his ticket and he held a kind of thieves honor in the accomplishment as he got off at what looked like the city center to him. There were giant cathedrals and plazas, it looked like a place he would be able to find some answers.

The big duffle bag fit perfectly onto his shoulders along with the backpack on his back, allowing him to hold the little duffle bag. He drugged through the city like this, going to every bank he could along his route. He stopped at several with the same result. He spoke to a teller at one of the banks once it opened. The banker informed Charlie there is no access to savings accounts in Belgium and in Europe as far as he knew. He suggested Charlie get some money sent to him via Western Union.

The teller explained to him how to get to the office. Charlie knew there would be a problem in getting in contact with anyone as he didn't have a cell phone. He asked the clerk when he arrived at the office if he could use a phone anywhere to get in contact with his family. She told him he could not use their phone, but the library had computers he could use to contact family or friends that way.

Charlie lugged his belongings to the great library nothing like any he'd seen before, guarded by two colossal stone lions at the entrance. When he went inside, he saw the grandeur before his eyes that was the library of Brussels. He knew he could spend eternity there and never get bored and he was sad he couldn't enjoy it in its full capacity because of the circumstance.

"I'm an American journalist traveling and have just arrived in Europe," he explained to the librarians, who he knew were his only hope. They knew it too by the way he was talking to them. "I've been unfortunately stranded from my money and need help getting in contact with my family to get some help. Would you wonderful librarians be so good as to help a poor American like me?"

The sweet librarians allowed Charlie to use the computers to contact his family free of charge. Charlie was able to message Emma, the Austrian nurse after gaining access to a computer through their sweet generosities. Emma gave Charlie her credit card number to buy a train ticket to Zurich where she would pick him up.

The only train leaving for Zurich was departing in 30 minutes. It was either catch the train or be stranded in Brussels for another day with nothing but a credit card number. When he went to purchase the train ticket, the only website selling the tickets was in German. Charlie didn't speak any German besides "gesundheit." He was forced to desperately enlist the help of the librarians. After some inquiry, it was determined one of them was German and could help Charlie purchase his ticket.

It was a small miracle for Charlie, as he deeply feared having to sleep in the street of Brussels.

Together, they were able to buy the ticket and print it out with only 20 minutes to spare until the train departed. Charlie thanked the lovely librarians and loaded his luggage onto his shoulder, back and hands, running out the doors of the famous library where he wished he could spend forever if it were not for the pesky things in life that deterred him.

He ran as fast as his feet could carry him without the luggage coming over his head on account of Charlie hunching down to bear the weight of the giant duffle bag on his shoulders. His shoulders began to ache with the enormous weight of all his belongings bearing down on him. He kept a steady pace and watched the time as he hurried to meet the oncoming train and his destiny in Zurich.

When he entered the station he had difficulty finding where his train was going to come in due to everything being in Flemish. He made out Zurich and quickly made his way to the terminal as he had four minutes to spare. He arrived at the gate with less than a minute to spare as the train pulled into the station and he boarded knowing it barely avoided being stranded in Brussels for the evening.

Charlie immediately fell asleep, sleeping for hours before he was awakened by French officials demanding to see his passport. Charlie groggily looked around at all the passengers looking at him and his luggage with an air of suspicion.

He dug through his luggage to produce the precious document to the French officials as they patiently waited. He handed them his ticket first and they handed it back as he then produced his worn passport. They looked it over with an air of suspicion, but after finding nothing of a criminal nature in his conduct, handed it back to him and then got off the train. He was only to pass through France for a small portion of the seven-hour trip, but he managed to get checked by French officials in his short and only time in France, even though he was asleep.

The train moved on through the countryside as Charlie drifted back to sleep, wondering how he was going to manage through this adventure with no money.

"It will all work out," he thought to himself. "It always has and always will. Worrying will only make it worse and isn't going to make a thing better."

The sun set over the late winter horizon, Charlie's first sunset on the continent. He watched it fade away and the lights of Zurich slowly come into view. He knew meeting up with Emma would be the difficult part without a cell phone to tell her where to meet him, but she was there waiting for him when his train came into the station.

"I was worried you weren't going to find me," Charlie said to her smiling from ear to ear. "I don't think I could have handled another setback right now. Thank you for rescuing me."

"It's not exactly how I envisioned we would meet again," she said to him coolly. "But you made it to me like you said you would in California."

Charlie and Emma met at the hostel in San Diego. She was on holiday to the United States for three weeks and ended her stay in San Diego to learn how to surf. She got in a few sessions while she was there and sparked up a platonic romance with Charlie.

Charlie being easily taken by beautiful women was seduced by the Austrian nurse with little effort. He vowed the night before she left for Austria to come visit in her home country. She didn't believe him. Emma was more taken by the fact he was uncircumcised than anything else.

"Are you Jewish," she asked him.

"No, that's just what they do here in America when you're born, I think," he responded. "Do they not circumcise the men in Austria?

"None that I've seen," she said.

The two kept in contact throughout the time Charlie was in the Dominican Republic, all the while telling him not to drink too much. He didn't listen to her but told her he would.

When the opportunity presented itself in the form of a cheap ticket to Brussels from Davey, Charlie pounced on the opportunity to come and visit Emma. He stayed there with her and her family for several months. They celebrated Fasching in March, which Charlie compared to Mardi Gras. Slowly Charlie began to be more interested in Emma's friends than her and she grew tired of waiting for his money to wire transfer from his bank. Emma lent him money until it came in, a little after a month of his arrival.

They would go on hikes to the castles in the hills just behind Emma's family estate. They would walk the broken ruins, talking of what they wanted out of life. They fundamentally disagreed on several issues but were drawn together by how similar they were to each other. Neither were prepared to make the relationship into something more and after spending three months in Austria with Emma, Charlie got on a train at the Feldkirch Railway station, headed for Spain.

Charlie gazed at the quote in Austrian above the ticket counter from James Joyce. In English, it translated to, "Over there, on those tracks, the fate of Ulysses was decided in 1915." It was the place where Joyce later said the fate of Ulysses was decided.

Charlie tried to imagine what it would be like to be persecuted because of being a writer. He would have to find a way back home eventually, there were only sights in Europe to see and there was no home to be had there. He wanted things to be different and find the thing he was looking for. He knew he would have to go back to the states, but he had no idea what he was going to do when he got there. It was 2014, and he thought anything was possible.

Ka Kauai kauwela

Charlie picked up The Sir at Lihue international airport on June 6th, 2019. It had been five years since they said their good-byes in the Dominican Republic. After their time in the Dominican, The Sir went back to San Diego and took Charlie's old job as the hostel manager. He worked there for years until getting into a motorcycle accident that left him with a limp and permanent disability. He collected a monthly check for the limp, so he didn't mind it much. In fact, it better provided for his lifestyle, which mostly consisted of late nights and no working.

Charlie had gone to Austria after he left the Dominican Republic, looking for love before realizing it was not what he wanted. He headed to Spain hoping to recapture some of the magic he and The Sir had created in California and the Dominican Republic, but was never able to and ran out of money. He got a ticket back to the states and ended up on the East Coast before meeting Aubrey in Denver. She enchanted him from their first meeting and saved his life when he attempted to move to Costa Rica permanently and was drinking too much. He found out she was pregnant when he was getting arrested at customs coming back into the states.

It was a rocky road after that. Charlie did all he could once he got out and things were cleared up for a few years. Aubrey could never trust him again no matter how hard she tried to. He didn't blame her for that. Eventually, he found a niche in journalism, traveling to all the small towns that made up his familiar west. After a few of these campaigns, the pair grew apart. Aubrey looked at Charlie as expendable outside of the money he provided from working in faraway places.

Aubrey wouldn't let him see his son as things got worse between them. Charlie grew angrier over time before leaving to the

Four Corners to run a small newspaper in San Juan County. When things eventually fell apart like they always seemed to for Charlie, he got a chance to come to Kauai and serve the community as a weekend editor.

Knowing it was a once in a lifetime opportunity, Charlie broke the news to Aubrey he would be leaving for the island. He visited her and Joyce in Wyoming, who was turning three that year, leaving her money and the promise he would make a life for them in paradise.

That was how Charlie entered into what he thought was going to be an endless summer, but as things continued to fall apart in his relationship with Aubrey, he realized he was going to lose his family.

The time in Kauai went by in the blink of an eye as the spring turned to summer and the temperature heated up. In April Charlie covered Mark Zuckerberg buying up nearly 700 acres of Kuleana land creating contention on the island against the sale. Zuckerberg forced the land nearby his already owned parcels to be auctioned, even if they were owned by local families. The auction took place on the courthouse steps.

Every reporter and photographer on staff at the paper went to the auction. Only two of them were sent there on assignment, but Charlie got the idea to broadcast the auction on Facebook live.

"If I use his own system to broadcast the auction live, the universe is going to consume itself," he told Daniel.

Charlie got as close as he could for the start of the auction and held his phone front and center to record it. Angry Hawaiians chanted different variations of, "haole" and carried signs proudly condemning the auction as an illegal land grab.

Mark Zuckerberg was not in attendance, but his lawyers were and they did the bidding for him so he would not have to hear the chants face to face.

One by one, parcels of land were auctioned off and Zuckerberg bought them, less one parcel he was outbid on. The family that outbid him paid $700,000 for a parcel of land they already owned.

The next morning, Charlie landed on the front page of the

Honolulu Star Advertiser. He was holding his phone recording the auction like a tourist. The local television station in Honolulu called the newspaper and requested to use the footage that Charlie had broadcast live on Facebook.

Charlie's editor granted the television station the right to use the footage excitedly and later condemned Charlie for going to the auction without permission. After he berated Charlie and made sure that he understood who was in charge, told him good job. It was the first time Charlie had been told he was doing a good job since he got there and it came with a scolding.

In late April, Charlie uncovered a homeless camp in the center of the Lihue, across from the mayor's office. It hid in plain sight and Charlie discovered it was on Department of Transportation land after receiving an anonymous tip from a lawyer representing the old sugar mill trust which was the property adjacent to the camp, a fact the government seemed to be unaware of. Charlie published a series of articles on the camp, not understanding how the government would respond.

He hoped it would usher in a new era of understanding and helping, but he was still young and didn't realize there is no money to be made in that form of humanitarianism.

The last article in the serires read— "In what is the start of an islandwide homeless encampment sweep, government agencies began removing unauthorized property and persons on a parcel of state land along Rice Street Wednesday morning.

The sweep near the Haleko Shop Complex was the second stage of removing the encampment which has been there for months, according to the Department of Transportation. The first stage was on April 17, when notices were posted to vacate under the possibility of receiving citations.

Authorities began moving in about 8:30 a.m., according to Homeless Director Jun Yung, who flew in from Oahu to oversee operations.

Renae Wa'alani, house manager and intake coordinator with Women In Need, who runs a home for women and children and does outpatient treatment and domestic violence classes, was on hand to offer assistance while local contractors, HTM, took apart the encampment.

"We gave the women our cards so they can come to our office if they need help," Wa'alanai said. "So that's what we do. There's a procedure you have to go through to get into the house. They can start from there if they want the help."

For some business owners at the Haleko complex, the removal of the encampment came as a surprise, but with some relief.

Kauai Community Health Center employees watched through the windows of the Lihue community health center as the DOT and Kauai police took apart the complex, piece by piece, which has caused problems for the businesses in the area.

"It's gonna be safer," one employee said, who preferred not to be named. "It's only because our employees work after dark and these people come when we're closed, which makes it a little scary."

Jung said the operation met little resistance.

"Everybody's been peaceful, it's just a matter of giving plenty of time to figure out what they want to do with their items," Yung said. "That this is going to happen and have plenty of service providers to give them services."

Yung said from his last report from the Kauai Economic Opportunity Wednesday morning, there were 11 beds available at the KEO shelter, which has a total of 19 beds. He said they encountered around "four or five people" who were still in the encampment.

DOT and Yang plan to remove encampments under the Wailua Bridge, the Pua Loke Arboretum, and eventually along the shores of Ahukini Landing. There is one known occupant under the Wailua Bridge, who is a veteran, according to Yang.
"It would be great to see him move into housing, and they have housing options," he said."

The homeless people blamed Charlie for the raid and yelled at him the day it happened while he was taking pictures. Deep down Charlie felt like if he hadn't written anything the government probably wouldn't have taken action. But once the public was alerted, the government responded by destroying the homeless camps on the island, including the one near the airport Charlie discovered when he first came onto the island.

It was the first time the authorities had taken this form of action against the homeless population on the island of Kauai. Public sentiment was the people who resided in the camp were not from Hawaii and Charlie started to hear rumblings other states were paying their homeless to get on a flight to Hawaii. He searched diligently for the paper trail to any evidence that would support these rumblings but always fell just short of obtaining it.

As a catch to receiving the tip from the lawyer, Charlie was required to meet with another local lawyer, notorious for having represented Henry Noa. Noa was the "Prime Minister" of the Kingdom of Hawaii. He aimed to occupy kuleana lands and slowly start to regain land for the rightful kingdom of Hawaii. He saw Hawaii as a lost kingdom that has been illegally occupied by the United States since 1898.

Charlie met with Stan Hempy, the local lawyer who represented Noa ten years prior when he was arrested for attempting to occupy Kahoolawe, a small island in the Hawaiian archipelago near Maui the US Navy used to test bombs on until 1990.

Noa was due to arrive on Kauai by May and Hempy wanted Charlie to interview him and cover the three meetings he was going to present. Hempy convinced Charlie the kind of revolutionary material Noa was presenting had never been written about before. Hempy gave Charlie Noa's number and Charlie pitched the idea to his editor, who to Charlie's surprise, loved the idea.

"We haven't written anything about Kahoolawe or Noa in years," his editor told him. "That sounds fantastic, Charlie."

During these events that were beginning to shape Charlie's time on the island, he had managed to make a deal with Joel Fryer in April to move into a house he was renovating. It was a giant mansion dilapidated to the point of needing to be either torn down or completely rebuilt. Charlie assumed the master suite in the house after working there for a few weeks, helping to whip it back into a liveable condition.

In the center of the dilapidated villa was a pool a quarter full of root beer colored water that served as a breeding ground for mosquitoes and cane toads.

Fryer chose to rebuild the house using only work-trade labor and one carpenter he paid modestly for his service.

In addition to the mosquitoes and cane toads, a lonely bullfrog had found his way into the pool. At night Charlie would wake up to the frog's lonely echoed and amplified cries for a mate, thinking them to be some strange alien creature in the depths of the dark.

In the last week of April, Jason invited Charlie to a dinner party. Jason had been seeing a Canadian girl who was recently widowed after her husband died in Jerusalem in service of the Canadian special forces.

"Her name is Erin, Charlie," Jason said to him. "She just bought a house on the Westside about a week ago and she's having a little house warming party. It's not going to be anything big, just dinner and a few drinks. Come over and have a few beers with us."

Charlie, just getting off work from putting the Sunday paper together, jumped at the idea of socializing outside the groups of tent people living at Fryer's villa. Tent people was the term Charlie created to describe people who lived in tents on the property. They didn't last long before finding better living arrangements in general, but some would last.

He made the long drive to the Westside of the island from Lihue, which takes just over an hour to get to the warmest and driest part of the island. It was also the least gentrified and still held an air of what was the old Hawaii.

When Charlie got to Erin's house, Daniel met him at the driveway and rolled away the gate so he could park.

"Glad you found it, Charlie," he said, greeting him with a shaka. "You made it just in time too. Dinner just got finished."

There was Erin, Daniel, a young couple, and a woman who caught Charlie's eye. She was vibrant and beautiful as a Hawaiian flower and as fragrant. Charlie couldn't help but stare at her and she noticed.

They made polite conversation after dinner as they sat around the lanai enjoying the cooler evening air.

"So Jason says you're the political reporter," Erin said to Charlie. "That must be pretty interesting right? I bet you get to talk to all kinds of people."

"Sometimes," he responded. "Mostly just homeless people and government officials. It depends on the day."

"How old are you," Erin's roommate asked Charlie with an air of intrigue.

"Old enough to know better and old enough not to return the question," he responded.

"I'm Sarah, Charlie," she said, smiling. "It's good to meet you. I'm glad you came to our little housewarming party."

The young couple who came for dinner left first, leaving Daniel, Charlie, Erin, and Sarah to their evening. Sarah suggested a walk to the beach to, "hear the ocean."

Charlie, not wanting to face the long drive across the island just yet, decided to join her.

She brought a blanket to lay on the sand along with a couple of cold beers. Daniel and Erin decided to come along and they brought a blanket of their own to lay on the sand. Charlie and Sarah walked ahead of the other two, talking about their lives on the island and back home. Charlie kept out the part about his son.

"I work at the only hospital on the Westside," Sarah said to him. "It's really been a dream of mine to live in Hawaii my whole life and here I am. It's kind of crazy it happened this way."

"Could you ever imagine yourself going back?" Charlie asked her, asking the same question to himself internally.

"I try to go back to the mainland at least once a month," she said, looking into his eyes. She liked his eyes. "If you don't go back, you start to get island fever."

"I haven't left since I got here," Charlie said. "It's been three months now. How long before you start to get island fever?"

"Do you have an island girlfriend?" she asked Charlie while she was laying the blanket out on the beach. He looked at her, the moon rising over the whole of the island. He knew she had a beautiful friendly soul.

"No," he answered, sitting down next to her. He was close enough to feel the anticipation, something he hadn't felt in a long time and forgotten.

They spent the rest of the evening talking on the beach, walking down it slowly after they tired of sitting. When it was time for them to go, Charlie built up the nerve and finally asked her.

"It's a really long drive home across the island," he said. "Would it be too much trouble if I spent the night here and drove home in the morning?"

She smiled at him and simply said, "I would like that."

The next morning, Charlie awoke fresh and full of life. Sarah had to work a shift at the hospital early and he didn't want to wake her, but also wanted her to know he wanted to see her again, so he left his business card on the kitchen counter. She awoke shortly after he left, a little sad he'd left so early without saying goodbye. She smiled when she saw the card sitting on the counter.

"That's the same thing I did with Erin," Daniel said to Sarah, drinking his coffee in the living room.

"What is the same thing you did?" Sarah responded.

"Left my card the next morning. It's a good move. It shows he means business. You know, in a business sense?"

Sarah didn't know and went about her day thinking of the night before and the possibility of a new romance in her life. It had been such a long time since she felt like she met someone who she truly connected with and wanted to spend time getting to know. She was cognizant of her age, knowing she was not getting any younger.

Paradise is better sharing it with somebody you love, she thought to herself.

She hoped Charlie would call her, but she didn't hold her breath. She thought about these things during her shift as an ICU nurse on the Westside of the garden island. She had a wonderful life there, but something was missing. She couldn't help thinking that something might be a man like Charlie.

Charlie left that morning and took the short drive from their house to Polihale. He had visited there once before when he wrote an article about World War 2 troop carriers that washed up on the beaches of Polihole near Queens Pond after a winter storm moved the sands. There are four of them that wash up every ten years or so when a strong enough winter storm hits and the beach sands shift. The carriers sit there year after year, some badly decomposed, but one nearly intact.

In the article, Charlie wrote about a family of tourists who happened upon the carriers after one of these storms exposed them. They were amazed at what they saw and thought they were the ones who discovered them. Charlie, not knowing himself, wrote the article as if the family had actually discovered the troop carriers and the response to the article was immense. Although he took his lumps with the article, it brought attention to the fact the army abandoned the carriers there prior to launching into the depths of the Pacific theater. The carriers broke down during mock amphibious invasion drills and the army buried them on the beach and went about winning the war. Time went on and the sands devoured them, only to be washed up every so often.

Charlie spent the entire morning exploring Polihole. He thought about how he was going to take his friends camping there and how he would love to spend time with Sarah in that place. He thought about his evaporating relationship with Aubrey and how everything he tried seemed to make things worse.

He still loved the mother of his child, but he knew she couldn't love him the way he needed to be loved. There were things within his soul she couldn't fathom, let alone understand and nurture. The same was true for Charlie. He began to feel so far removed from her both physically and mentally that he wondered if he could ever get any of it back.

The thought of losing his child or going through a nasty custody battle weighed heavy on his mind. Aubrey loved Wyoming and being near her family too much to ever leave. Charlie had long outgrown the Cowboy state. There was so much outside a life lived staying in one place to him. No matter how he tried, he could never be comfortable with the possibility of living in that one place for the rest of his life. The thought of it drove him mad. He knew he had to make a choice when he lived there with Aubrey long ago. It took him years to be honest with himself about how he felt living there so long ago. It made him cringe to think about going back and living there.

A few days after meeting Sarah, he flew to Honolulu on assignment to cover the inaugural flight of a double engine propeller plane service from Princeville on the north side of the Kauai to Honolulu on Oahu. The "Kanaka Air" service as it was dubbed, had run five years prior but abruptly stopped when one of the planes crashed into the ocean and a passenger on the plane died of a heart attack floating and waiting for rescue. To add insult to injury, the person who died was the director of the Hawaii Department of Health.

The family sued the air service and the charming CEO, resulting in the cancelation of their flight from Princeville to Honolulu for over half a decade.

Charlie got the opportunity to cover the flight after winning a coin flip with Daniel. Their editor told them about the story, pitting them against each other to sort out who would cover it. They went out into the parking lot and made terms of how a coin flip would determine who got to go on assignment.

"How about we do one flip and that decides it," Daniel suggested to Charlie, who in turn agreed and flipped the coin as he was the designated flipper. "Tails."

It came down and slowly revealed the coin had landed on heads.

"Best two out of three," Daniel demanded.

"Not a chance, I'm going to Honolulu," Charlie said gleefully, lighting up a celebratory American Spirit. "Thanks for calling tails though. Who does that?"

"I do it every time," he said, defending his decision. "It's something I've always done since I was a kid. Usually, win with it."

"You know that heads has a better chance statistically right? It's something like fifty-one percent to forty-nine. It's mathematically a better bet, but I'm glad you stuck to your guns on this one."

"Oh well. You do know the last time this flight ran it crashed into the ocean?" Daniel said, laughing in between the puffs of his cigarette.

"I didn't know that, but now I do," Charlie said matter of factly, thinking over if he should write out a living will before he boarded the plane.

Charlie never made a living will after winning the right to cover the inaugural flight. The deciding factor was he didn't have anything to begin with, so whoever he left a will out to would inherit nothing but debt. He prayed instead a few nights before the flight on May 1, which is known as May Day, something that didn't appease Charlie's fears, that he would make it to Honolulu safe and sound in one piece so he could return home to his son someday.

Sarah called him at work the day before he left.

"Lava man," she said to him through the office phone at Charlie's desk in the newsroom when he answered the unfamiliar number. "You left me your card and I couldn't let you down not using it. I just wanted to say I had a great night with you and I want to do it again. I'll even make dinner."

"I did too," Charlie replied. "I think we both needed a night like that. It would be good to do it again. I'll bring something this time."

She agreed and they arranged a time to meet when he returned on island. Charlie thanked her for calling and wished her a good day, almost smelling her southern sweetness through the phone.

The morning of the flight, Charlie made his way to the northern side of the island where the plane would be landing at 9 a.m. He was early. Something he tried not to be in Hawaii, but the sheer excitement of flying over the Hawaiian archipelagos excited him and prompted him out of bed that morning.

When the twin-engine landed on the runway with a group of people amassed to greet the arrival, including a Hawaiian Medicine Man who was there to bless the plane and its first voyage from Kauai to Oahu. There were words spoken of admiration and excitement by the CEO, who upon the conclusion of his speech, approached Charlie and began to ask him questions about Daniel's article which had painted the airline and the crash five years prior in a poor light.

"We weren't interested in rehashing the past and we still aren't," Tom Hanson, the CEO told Charlie.

"I'm not interested in the past either, sir," Charlie responded. "In fact, I dislike the past altogether and attempt daily to remove it from my life and circle."

"I couldn't believe he went in such depth about the woman who died and the negligence and this and that," Tom said. "It was disappointing. I was looking forward to laying it on the author and am a little disappointed you're not this Daniel guy. What's your name?"

"Charlie Porter, government reporter and weekend editor at your service, Tom. Now let's talk about what you're going to do with this air service and connecting the Hawaiian Islands."

For the rest of the afternoon, Tom and Charlie were rubbing shoulders. Charlie was way out of his league hanging with millionaires who cared nothing of him or his ambitions, but only saw what they had a vision for. Charlie, to Tom was a tool to use to get what he wanted and hopefully to get some good free publicity.

Charlie, on the other hand, wanted to make friends and have the opportunity to make a better life for himself at some point rather than just hash it out with CEOs who always told you what you wanted to hear and were so dreadfully boring with their ambitions and flowing money. He marveled at Pearl Harbor as the plane dropped altitude on its landing approach.

"How could a military mind bottle our entire fleet like that in such a small harbor?" Charlie asked Tom rhetorically. "That man should have been taken out back and shot."

When Tom showed Charlie around the Honolulu terminal which was small, but new, he told him to give him a call if he needed anything. And with that he was gone, never to be seen by Charlie again.

Charlie and a magazine owner were the only two remaining from the inaugural flight and required a lift back to the small Kauai airport outside of Princeville. The two pilots, Charlie, and the magazine owner began their trek back to the garden island and carried on a semi-interesting conversation.

"I reached a point where I just had to do my own thing," the magazine owner told Charlie. "It gets old listening to editors and publishers that only care about the advertising money and don't care about making a difference in the community or any of that stuff. Some of these guys could make some real change if they wanted to. The problem is, they have become politicians like all the rest and don't want to do the actual work."

"Couldn't have said it better myself," Charlie responded. "How did you end up in Hawaii anyway then?"

"I came here in the 80s and never left," he said. "I was one of many that did it then and I wouldn't live anywhere else in the world. It's paradise. You're lucky you got here so young."

As they approached the runway, the plane encountered heavy cloud cover. So much so, the pilots had to rely on their instruments to navigate as they missed the first attempt at a landing. They circled three times before on the third go-around, they dove through the clouds and banked sharply as the runway came into view, narrowly adjusting in time to make the landing.

The white-faced pilots got a heartfelt "thank you" from Charlie and the magazine owner as they scurried off the plane.

As May progressed and Charlie celebrated Cinco De Mayo and Mother's Day with Sarah, they realized the love they had for each other and wanted to be together. For Charlie it was a relief and a problem as he still had not told Aubrey he'd met Sarah and he possibly was madly in love with her. Aubrey and Charlie were already on the rocks and with the child custody situation uncertain, Charlie knew when he told her there would be no alternative to a custody battle. It would be the final straw in the line of many many straws.

"She leaves you no choice, Charlie," Sarah said to him on Mother's Day when Charlie was particularly down. "If she were a little more open to allowing you to see him then maybe, but she's not going to do that. She won't let you see him until you have that piece of paper that says you get to see him."

"You're right, Sarah," he admitted not wanting her to be right. "I've tried everything I could and sometimes it just doesn't work out no matter how much you want it to or how hard you try to make it work. The only thing that scares me is the finality of it. Once you start down the path of a custody battle you have to go through it until it's over. And it's never really over."

"If you don't do it now, then you're going to have to do it down the road," she said to him. "And when you do it down the road, it's going to be harder on him, you, and her. If you want to be in his life then you have to file."

Charlie reluctantly agreed and in early June he filed papers in Wyoming for full custody for his son. He called Aubrey before with one last attempt to resolve the situation amongst themselves.

"We loved each other and had some amazing times, Aubrey, but you don't want to leave there and I don't want to make you. I want you to have what you want and be happy and thrive and you're happier without me."

"There's nothing more to talk about then is there, Charlie?" she said, hanging up the phone.

"It certainly will be talked about more," Charlie said to himself, shaking his head knowing what was to come in the next year.

One night in late June, Charlie, Sarah, Erin, and Daniel had a "staycation" at a local resort on the North Shore in Hanalei. They were taking in the evening and having a good time when a confused looking man crossed paths with Charlie on the beach.

"Come hang out with us, it's lonely to wander the beach alone at this time of night," Charlie said to the stranger walking past him. The stranger took up Charlie's invitation and in no time Charlie was introducing the man with a heavy Russian accent to the group.

"My name is Vlad Sukhoparov and I have just arrived from Russia," he said to the group. "I'm here to reestablish the Russian fort on the Westside of the island. Do you know of it?"

"We know of it," Charlie said to Vlad. "How are you going to reestablish the fort?"

"I am going to use some of our political influence and persuade the local politicians to our cause," Vlad proclaimed. "It's a very important mission for Moscow and they have sent me here to do the job.”

“I wouldn’t go around saying that to people Vlad,” Charlie suggested. “It may be that you find it dangerous to say a thing like that here.”

“My nickname is the Orca,” he said.

“Killer whale?” Daniel asked.

“I do not like the name, but it was given to me,” Vlad said. “Do you know any of the local officials here? It seems as if you are locals here.”

“We’re not locals. But some may think they are,” Sarah said, casting a look in Daniel’s direction.

“Vlad, you should come with us to the gay pride parade tomorrow,” Charlie suggested.

“Gay pride parade, what do you mean?” he asked.

“It’s a festival for people to celebrate their pride. It’s the first in Kauai’s history this year, you might like it,” Charlie said.

The look of horror on Vlad’s face gave the impression he was not in favor of attending. With an immediate decline of the invitation, Vlad thanked them for their hospitality and advice and disappeared into the darkness of the night, followed by the sounds of crashing waves verberating through the air.

The next morning Charlie and Daniel went to work to find a press release the coast guard was looking for a man named Vladimir Sukhoparov, reported missing that morning by his wife after not returning from his morning run. Search and rescue crews found Vlad’s sandals on the beach but did not locate the man with the thick Russian accent who claimed to be sent from Moscow to the group the night before. The press release said Vlad was visiting from Ohio with his wife.

Two days later after the Coast Guard scoured the area for any signs of the missing man, the search was called off.

Sarah and Erin were taken back by the news and wondered openly if there was more behind the disappearance than what was being reported.

“He was a Russian spy who said the wrong thing to someone. That or the 11-foot waves crashing down on the beach that morning did the trick. Either way, I’ve never heard of something so strange as this," Charlie said to them.

The situation to Charlie reeked of having to do with a series of articles he'd just published in the paper about a local councilwoman. She'd recently taken a trip to Russia to be a delegate for the new designation of the Russian fort near where James Cook made his initial landing on Kauai in 1778. Just next to the Waimea River mouth. He was the first European to have gazed eyes on the Hawaiian islands according to some histories.

Alone, the girls wondered if Charlie had something to do with it because he was the one who called Vlad over to the group. Sarah defended Charlie as she felt inclined to do and they decided collectively as a group of friends it was a freak accident and weird happenstance. They also decided he was most definitely a Russian spy and someone had drowned him or threw his body in the ocean after murdering him brutally.

Erin began to think the girls may be in danger due to Daniel and Charlie's presence and voiced her concerns. Charlie told her there was no imminent danger unless he butchered a political article or did a hit piece on a powerful local. Daniel assured her she was in no danger despite the fact there were "lots of criminals" who would like to meet him in a dark alley for the articles he wrote about them.

"I've never been in harm's way or taken threats of any kind without dishing them out myself," he proclaimed, standing tall with all his stature.

By July, a massive protest against the biggest telescope in the world being built on Hawaii island erupted on all the Hawaiian islands. Moana Kea became the tipping point for many local Hawaiians who were tired of seeing their sacred lands desecrated.

Many disagreed, pointing to the fact there were already nearly a dozen telescopes atop the often snow-covered mountain. Protesters blocked traffic in Honolulu and native Hawaiians took up the call, coming together in a show of unity and strength against what they saw as injustice. The mayor and chief of police held a "listening meeting" Charlie covered for the newspaper.

It was like nothing Charlie had ever seen as angry people expressed their discontent with the government and their handling of the situation. It was a proactive move by the mayor, who Charlie had done a "Talk Story" with, which was a segment in the Sunday paper where one person was featured at length as they sat down and talked story with the reporter. This mayor had ambition and surfed, making him one of Charlie's favorite politicians to work with during his young career that had featured a one on one interview with Mitt Romney during his Utah senate race, (something Charlie's younger self would have denied) and the great-grandson of Theodore Roosevelt.

The mayor was effectively getting in front of the situation before it got out of hand. Charlie took a picture of a young man draped in a Hawaiian flag that landed on the centerfold front page of the paper the next morning. The man spoke of how his mother was shamed for speaking Hawaiian when she was growing up and was often punished for speaking it. He told of how he was not taught the language but now his sons were being taught the language in school, something he wished he had growing up.

"I'm scared for my culture," he told mayor Derek S. Kawakami and the new chief of police, freshly arrived from Las Vegas where he held the same post.

Charlie witnessed the message of Henry Noa coming to life in the form of discontent and a feeling of their land being stolen from them and held since 1898. The "movement" was continuing to grow and it had erupted into a fight over the Thirty Meter Telescope as it was named and abbreviated to TMT for convenience sake.

He had been told and read how the islands were united under the warrior king Kamehameha, forming the Kingdom of Hawaii. One local told Charlie that Kamehameha was seven feet tall and killed dozens leading up to the unification of the Hawaiian islands under his leadership in the late 1700s and early 1800s. Charlie was told how they were a proud kingdom that was eventually overtaken at gunpoint by American businessmen when they forced Queen Liliuokalani against her will to abdicate the throne after being arrested and placed under a military tribunal who convicted her of treason. She was sentenced to be imprisoned in her house and formally turned over the Hawaiian Kingdom to the foreign rebels on January 25, 1895.

All of that mattered to the local kanaka whose distant relatives descended from such ordeals, but with each passing generation their numbers dwindled and their blood diluted. The majority of the local Hawaiians were of second-generation blood who came to Hawaii looking for a better life. Be it from the Philippines, Japan, the outer pacific rim, they now held a collective belief tourism was the problem, despite their livings being made from such enterprises. The racism at times was palpable to the haole such as Charlie and Daniel.

The governor of Hawaii ordered the National Guard to destroy the camps the protestors built. The protesters held steadfast, blocking the road to Mauna Kea and the other 13 telescopes already in existence at the summit. Their presence kept the construction from commencing on the telescope, forcing the project's leaders to look to other locations as possible alternatives. The battle lasted throughout the Hawaiian summer or kauwela as it's called in Hawaiian.

By August, Daniel and Sarah broke off their relationship. Sarah was from Canada and did not work, she had a hefty check from the Canadian government each month. She received the check after her late husband, who was in the Canadian military, died under mysterious circumstances in Jerusalem while on active duty. She never knew what happened to her husband who she had only been married to for a couple of months before he left her to go on deployment, something she had a bad feeling against and begged him not to do.

She was set for life and didn't need to work to make a living, but needed to do it to keep herself occupied, or at least that's what her friend Sarah thought of the situation. Because Erin didn't work, she never got an American visa and could only stay for a few months before having to go back home or abroad until she could come back. She fought the situation legally instead of getting a job that granted her a visa.

"A job would just slow me down," she would tell Sarah while smoking a joint, something she did every half hour. "I'm just going to have to go home until Christmas, and then I can come back again once the year is over."

With this prospect of having to go back to Canada for four months, Erin asked if Sarah would mind taking care of the responsibilities that came with her house.

Sarah accepted the task and excitedly told Charlie the news one afternoon.

"We will have the whole house to ourselves," she said to him. "The rent will be cheap and all you will have to do is maintain the yard or something like that to keep her happy."

"I've been thinking about it Sarah and I think I'm going to have to go back to the mainland," Charlie said to her, looking deep into her perplexed blue eyes.

"Why would you ever want to do something crazy like that?"

"I don't think I'm going to be able to fight this custody battle here in Hawaii, Sarah. There's no way in hell they would ever let me see the boy here. I've broken the news about us to Aubrey and it has just compounded the situation. She won't let me see Joyce here on the island, she's said as much. Her offer was for me to come back and visit him on the mainland. She's refusing to let him come to Hawaii."

"Damn that girl," Sarah said. "To hell with her. Fight it from afar, Charlie. You will regret it for the rest of your life if you leave and don't stay here in heaven on earth. This is the best it will get. I'm telling you."

"I know it is, Sarah," he said. "But if I don't go and fight this thing and do everything in my power, I will always regret that too. And I know myself. If I don't do everything I can then I will never be able to be happy."

"That's just in your mind," Sarah responded. "It will take a little time, but everything changes and there will be a point where he will be here with you."

"I don't think I can wait that long, Sarah," he said. "I have to be near him. I dream about him almost every night now. When I wake up it's this dream that gnaws at my insides and tears me up in my mind. The thought is always there, on my mind. There's no getting rid of it. It's this fear I'm losing him for good."

Sarah moved closer to Charlie, putting her arm around him. "You're not losing him, Charlie. Life moves on and your life is moving on. It didn't work out between you two and that's all right. Most people don't work out, but there are the ones that do work out. I think that can be us."

"Everybody thinks they will work out until it doesn't and everything falls apart, Sarah," he said to her, resisting her comforts, trying to ride out the pain solo. "I thought my family was going to work out and everything was going to be some fairy tale ending, but that's not the way things are. Most people are selfish and will only go as far as they have to and then when it starts to get uncomfortable, that's the end of it."

"Can we promise each other here and now we won't end like that?"

Sarah looked into his eyes and saw her future. She saw the eyes of her children staring back at her. She saw what she always wanted to see but never had. She saw herself and all the beauty she ever hoped for. For her it was simple, she knew she had to be with him and she would go wherever he went, even if it meant leaving everything behind that she'd worked so hard to get. It made her sad to know he didn't want to have heaven. Instead, he wanted to knowingly go into hell. Why would anybody want to do that, she wondered.

"I can try, Sarah, but you're old enough now to know those kinds of promises are just a thing and don't hold any meaning. Life is crueler than that and you know it. I love you. Our love has been something I never thought could be this joyful, but you know I have a son. I'm sorry I have this obligation hanging over my head that came before we met and I wish that things weren't this complicated, but I can't just leave him behind. He's my soul, he's my everything. Without him, there's no love for you or loving anything."

"Charlie, you know I will come with you if you decide to go, but I want you to think about this and think it over good," she said. "Look around you. This is heaven. We've made it to the best place there is and to go back now would be turning our backs on the true heaven that exists here and now. There's nothing purer than this island and she loves us both. She doesn't love everybody, but she sure loves us."

"She loves you more, Sarah," Charlie said to her. "She never loved me. She just brought me here to show me that she is the best thing that exists, and can exist in this realm, but her only goal is to kill me."

Sarah just stared at him, knowing he was going to leave the island and there was nothing she could do. Once he left the island, it would never be the same there for her. There would be no sunset as bright, or coconut water as sweet. The poke would all taste sour and the tourists would just annoy her and make her think about all the times they had together chasing rainbows and swimming under and through waterfalls. Leaving the island would kill a part of her and she knew she would never recover from the love she felt on that island and from that island. It had always been kind to her and inviting since the day she landed.

The decision was made.

Charlie and her would fly to Colorado and then drive to Wyoming at the end of August to face whatever awaited them there. She would come back after and say goodbye to the island to get her things while he stayed and built a residence there for them. He told his coworkers, Joel Fryer, The Sir, Daniel, the editor, Henry Noah, and all his local friends who he'd come to kind of know goodbye. None of them really cared, except The Sir.

"The second you leave these desert islands, things always get better," The Sir told him. "That's the only thing that is certain in this situation. It happens every time I come to one of these islands to hang out with you. Then you end up leaving and I end up taking over everything you started and never came close to finishing."

They boarded the plane in late August and Sarah cried to herself as they got on, knowing what she was leaving behind and going forward to.

They had no idea they got to experience Hawaii in the last free form it was in before everything changed the next year. It would never again bristle with that many tourists for many years to come shortly after they left.

An introduction to the Cowboy State

Charlie and Sarah flew into Denver on that precipice of winter in the Rockies, holding hands. Optimistic about what the future held, wanting nothing more than the picture they had both painted for themselves as the solution to the evils that existed in the world. They both wanted so badly to continue their relationship and build on what they had created for themselves and one day a family of their own.

Charlie felt as if he was doing the right thing and Sarah believed she was following her heart, and in doing that, was also doing the right thing. It was hard for Charlie to say goodbye to the newspaper on the Garden Island that had accepted him as another transplant fresh off the boat. Sarah wasn't ready to say goodbye to the island yet and it was more complicated for her to leave her job at the hospital as a nurse. It was also in her nature to take time making decisions and she loathed shooting from the hip as Charlie Porter was known to do.

The plan was for Charlie to establish residency in Wyoming during the period leading up to the custody trial, however long a process that may be. He figured it would take something like a year for the trial, so he informed his attorney and Aubrey's attorney he was now a resident of Wyoming after Sarah and he found a small second level in an old victorian house to rent. Sarah called it the treehouse with the white French doors and tree canopy view, leading to a room full of windows looking out to the Big Horn Mountains and the white snow beginning to accumulate on their rocky peaks, even in August.

Charlie showed his new love the West he knew from so long ago like a distant smell from childhood, forgotten until it's discovered again. She promised to show him her South one day in return.

They went to Rocky Mountain National Park and marveled at the great heights in those powerful mountains gleaming surreal in the late summer morning sun. Sarah smiled the entire time gaining elevation, gazing at the river that cut through rock as hard as time, winding its way down to the Front Range.

He took her to Saratoga and then Thermopolis where Chief Washakie gifted those sacred healing waters to the people in perpetuity as a parting gift. They went to Yellowstone and saw wild animals who have their last sanctuary in a place where they are marveled at by hordes of tourists with cameras from every corner of the world, hoping to catch a glimpse of the wild that no longer exists.

They stayed in the Irma Hotel in Cody, Wyoming that was owned by Buffalo Bill. It was his hotel in the west, named after his beloved daughter who he gifted it to in order to avoid debtors later in his liofe.

After spending some time in Wyoming, they went to Deadwood, South Dakota. Charlie recreated the scene of Wild Bill Hickok getting shot in the back of the head while holding an ace eight of spades in his hands at the Saloon No. 10. In the evening streets just outside the famed saloon, actors played out the trial of Jack McCall, the man who committed the cowardly murder of one of the icons of the old west.

"Wild Bill never liked to turn his back to the door they say, but it was the only seat left at the poker table," Charlie explained to Sarah, as if he were there when it happened, if only in his mind. "Old jack came and shot him dead and poor old Wild Bill never saw it coming."

They went to his grave and meandered, alive, looking at the names of the other souls with Wild Bill in that cemetery.

Charlie tried to lay out his conceptualization of industrial tourism and what he surmised as to what Ed Abbey had figured out so long ago. He'd been reading the Monkey Wrench Gang since coming back to the West.

"If Ed had had it his way, there'd be no paved roads leading to the great places in the national parks and monuments. He thought there should be a single entrance with a parking lot big enough to fit all the people visiting from far and wide, handing out bikes free of charge. From there, small dirt paths would lead everywhere and people would have to ride a bike instead of paving over with roads and destroying the areas we're supposed to be protecting."

Charlie told her how he didn't think anything like that was possible, that it was just some idealistic dream that wouldn't ever make the kind of money industrial tourism generates. All those places he had seen, like Moab and Kauai and his native Colorado, worshipped the almighty dollar that was generated by motivating the masses to seek out their states.

"If you think about all the money made in the whole system by the family gearing up, getting in the recreational vehicle and road-tripping across America, it would make your head explode," he explained to Sarah. "You have to count all that fast food, gas station visits, mindless plastic junk they consume on the long journey to Yellowstone National Park from Akron, Ohio or whatever corner they crawl out of to come and see the great American West, just to catch a glimpse of a grizzly in one of the last places on earth they can exist in the wild. You add the average family expenditure up a few million times over and over and you create an economy. One worth destroying any sacred spot over. It's enough to sell the soul of the land for."

"The same thing happened to Kauai, Charlie," she said. "Look what has happened to all the sacred spots the people love there. It's all been desecrated and trampled on."

"It reminds me of the petroglyphs in San Juan County," Charlie reminisced. "There was always some idiot who felt it necessary to inscribe their initials next to an ancient artist's elk. Nothing like a giant J.R. next to something the ancients carved with a piece of flint 10,000 years ago. That's the whole trouble. You can't even find a place nice and peaceful, because there aren't any. You may think there is, but once you get there, when you're not looking, somebody will sneak up and write 'fuck you' right under your nose," he said.

"You're sounding a little like Holden Caufield, Charlie."

"I just want to find the place I belong because I belong there," he said to her. "I've felt like I've belonged in many places, but I've never been able to find that place I can just stay and have forever. I don't know, maybe that doesn't exist and is just some made-up fantasy. It's been something I've tried for a long time, to find my place."

"It's going to be hard, Charlie," she said to him. "There's no doubt this is going to test you to your limit. You've had to give up what you love doing and that's going to be hard for you to stomach. How are you going to go on day to day doing what you hate?"

"Just as long as I get to see my son and he has a room in my house, I think it will get me through the day, but I don't know what to do," he said, looking into her blue eyes. "I think that's part of my trouble, I've been trying to come up with the answer so long now that I forget there's more to life than just trying to solve the equation."

Charlie pulled into Sheridan late at night, just after the sun had gone down. Sarah had fallen asleep and was awoken by the jolt of the brakes as Charlie came to a stoplight in the small town named after Custer's commanding officer.

Aubrey had moved to Wyoming again with Joyce shortly after Charlie left for Hawaii to be closer to her family that lived there, particularly her mother. She also liked the custody laws that existed in Wyoming and personally knew many women who had been treated with the utmost advantage, if not blatantly given bias, in Wyoming. The legislation for custody laws in the state had not been revised since 1995.

Charlie hired a local lawyer from another nearby town to avoid the common clubhouse approach the lawyers who are familiar with each other often take. He chose a female lawyer to help boost his appeal from a friendly mother as to the tragedy that occurs when a father is removed from his son. He could hear her voice reigning down undeniable truths through the courtroom at Aubrey and her attorney, who Charlie had just recently learned the name of and the accompanying reputation as a young female shark, specialized in family law.

A quick search of Aubrey's lawyer while he was still in Hawaii revealed Charlie was in over his head. The panic began to sink in as he immediately looked into all the available attorneys in the nearby town of Buffalo, Wyoming, some 40 miles south of Sheridan where the civil case had been filed months earlier by Charlie.

He found one who said she would take the case and had at first glance appeared to be a reputable firm. Charlie made the arrangements to meet her hours before the temporary hearing scheduled for the last day in August. They were to meet in her office and Charlie relaxed as he sent her over all his evidence and things he thought were important to his new attorney. The firm drew up the representation agreement and Charlie had himself a lawyer. He began to relax a little knowing he was going into the first hearing with an attorney and not representing himself.

He thought about representing himself, but then remembered the adage, "the person who represents themself has a fool for a client."

Charlie scraped together all the money he could while he was still in Hawaii and paid half the retainer. The other half of the retainer was promised to be given by Charlie in increments of $500 as the custody battle progressed.

"Do you think it will cost more than $5,000," he asked his attorney during a phone conversation while he was still in Hawaii.

"It's going to cost a whole lot more than that. I can assure you," she responded, sending Charlie's mind into a freefall of panic about how he was going to afford to go about trying to win back any rights with his son.

He relaxed as he showed Sarah around the town, the little there was to show of it. Sheridan had a summer charm to it Sarah said she liked.

"I like all the flowers they put up around town," she said to him one morning before the temporary custody hearing. "It has a real nice feel to it."

"Just give it a winter," Charlie said. "It gets so brutal here in the dead of winter you won't believe it's possible to be that cold. It's something you wished you never experienced and want out of as soon as possible. It gets into your bones and stays for six months. The first snow usually comes in September and the last one falls in late May."

Sarah couldn't understand how Charlie got himself involved with a girl like Aubrey.

"We met in a bar in Denver when I was on an escapade with The Sir and another guy named Mickey," he told her, trying to explain how they met. "I was in a weird place in my life, to say the least, and I didn't think I could meet anyone. And then she walked into the bar when I was on about my third drink. Some guy I had met at the bar was her friend and he introduced us and we had an instant connection. She gave me her number and told me to call her if I was ever in Denver again. I didn't think I'd ever be in Denver again, but I had to come back almost immediately and I called her. When I left the next day, we kept in touch and when I went to Costa Rica, she had a grandpa die and left her a hefty inheritance, so she bought a ticket and came to see me. I was in a terrible sort, had been drinking way too much and just kind of drifting through life. She talked me into coming back to Denver and I decided to do it. When I went through customs, they arrested me for a connection to some murder I had no part of because they found my blood on a gun that was used to shoot some cowboy's balls off. He almost bled to death from the wound that turned out to be from Mickey, who went to jail for a long time. When they arrested me, Aubrey yelled at me that she was pregnant. It was one of the best and worst moments of my life."

Sarah held reservations the man she now held to marry could put himself in such a position as to go through all of those things. That wasn't the man she knew and she didn't understand how the man she knew now could get himself into such horrible situations. His judgment didn't seem that poor to her, but they had only known each other for over four months now. In the back of her head, she couldn't help but wonder if she was getting herself into a huge mess. That thought was quickly put down by Sarah's overwhelming capacity for hope and love.

The day of the temporary trial came and Sarah and Charlie

decided it best that he go into the hearing alone. They didn't want to give any bad impressions or make the situation worse than it was, so Sarah stayed home at the little "treehouse" apartment Charlie had found and rented to show he actually lived in the town now.

Charlie drove to the little town of Buffalo just south of Sheridan and walked into his lawyer's office. He was full of a sense of justice and the hope the system would work for him and grant him the ability to be a normal and constant part of Joyce's life.

When he arrived at the receptionist's desk and asked for his attorney, the look on the receptionist's face told the tale.

"We've been trying to call you all morning Mr. Porter," she said to him. "Your attorney isn't available to come to the temporary hearing this morning I'm afraid."

"What?" Charlie retorted in disbelief.

"The trial in Gillette yesterday got held over to today," the receptionist said to him codly, knowing full well Charlie's attorney just didn't want to go to the temporary hearing and delegated it to a new associate at the firm whom she had a grudge with. "Your attorney who will be representing you today is waiting for you in Sheridan now."

None of the documentation he'd submitted was ready or available to be used, so he raced through his phone, sending it all again. He was furious it would come down to go into the hearing after coming halfway across the world with an attorney he hadn't talked to. He knew this was more than just a coincidence, but he just kept going as he always did no matter how the hand was rigged against him.

The entire thing had been pre-arranged before Charlie even stepped foot into the courtroom, or at least that is how he felt when the 30-minute hearing to decide the fate of his son's next year was over.

It was over so fast, that Charlie had thought it had just begun, but it was decided he would receive "reasonable visitation" until a full day trial could be conducted in just under a year.

He was now able to see his son every other weekend and

the holidays were split.

He was ecstatic at first, thinking it was better than not seeing him at all like it had been the previous year. But as the days progressed, he realized he lived down the street and would be expected to toe the line while hardly seeing the boy at all.

"We're just here to get that piece of paper and then we're on to something else," Sarah would tell him. "There's nothing here we haven't faced before."

"I'm telling you, Sarah, there's nothing like Wyoming," he said in all seriousness. "There's a joke that it's not real. That it's just some figment of the imagination or grey area on the map you fly over on your way to better things. Once you spend a little time here, you'll understand."

"I think that's a part of your poor outlook on life, Charlie," she told him. "If you just give a little positivity maybe things will work out differently than the past. You have never been here with me before, so at least there's something different this time around."

In actuality, the mere fact the two were together in Wyoming drove Aubrey mad. It was the one thing Charlie could do to make her even more upset than she already was about him leaving and moving to Hawaii. It was a personal insult to Aubrey he brought Sarah to Wyoming and planned to make his living there until the trial.

It was then Aubrey decided she was going to fight his every step and do everything in her power to remove Charlie from the boy's life. Even if that meant casting as many spells as she could she looked up on Pinterest.

To Aubrey, Charlie was nothing more than a wrong decision in a life of wrong decisions, but none of that was her fault. It was a long line of problems associated with the flakey nature of men, starting with her father who abandoned her at a young age.

"Men are nothing more than temporary company," Aubrey told herself going through man after man once she and Charlie ended their relationship. "There's nobody out there who will feel passionate about me and accept my child as theirs. Damn Charlie for thinking he can just skip the hard parts and have fun. He shouldn't be able to enjoy the good part now. I've done all the work. To hell with him, I'll shed a few tears and scream abuse. No judge in the world will be able to deny it. I'll get him put in jail if I want."

To Aubrey, this was something that had to take place. She had no qualms with doing things her way and making Charlie have to live his life based on her decisions. If she felt compelled to let him see their son, which she never did, then she wanted to be respected and appreciated as doing good.

Charlie for his part, wanted to see his boy and nothing more. He missed him so much sometimes it made him feel as if he were slowly dying inside, painfully. It was missing the time together which inflicted the most damage to his psyche. He likened it to losing a family member. There was nothing more important in the world to Charlie than his son and he put everything in his life aside to come to Wyoming to seek the court as his advocate, hoping they would allow him to once again have any rights as a parent.

The stakes were set and after a year of fighting, now all Charlie had to do was follow the temporary order and not get into trouble. If he was able to do that then maybe, just maybe he told himself, he would be able to play a bigger role in his son's life at some point.

"I just don't understand it, Sarah," he said. "Why is it that they just automatically hand everything over to women in these circumstances? Isn't there supposed to be some kind of impartiality or something like that? It's ridiculous they ordered her to supervise our first visitation after withholding the boy for so long."

"I can't believe that," Sarah said. "They want to have the person who is responsible for taking him away from you supervise the first visit. That I just can't believe."

The judge, thinking he would rather be somewhere else during the 30-minute temporary hearing that day, decided it would be best for the child if he followed the standard procedure of ordering the father to receive bare minimum visitation. He did this out of experience, having known the impact of ordering the child to go with the father and he did it out of hope the family would work it out together and move on for the sake of the child.

Aubrey took the hearing as justification she was in the right and Charlie was clearly in the wrong. She dug in even more and resolved to make sure he would see his son as little as possible until the day she could muster tears on the stand and claim abuse. The judge set the trial out nine months from then and didn't think twice that night about what he'd ordered or the impact it would make in their lives. He fell asleep with a clean conscience that night as he always did. Tomorrow there would be more decisions for him to make and there was no crying over spilt milk in his book, which was a rather long book.

Charlie tossed and turned, thinking over all the possibilities in his mind, letting the thoughts race around his head over and over.

"I should have never let her take him from Utah," he told himself. "That's where I made the mistake. I let her take him from Utah and then it was all over. I had no options once she had physical possession of him. There was no hope for me getting primary custody once I let her take him."

Charlie kept this up for the better part of the night but was calmed by knowing he would see his boy the next day for the first time in seven months. It would be the start of a new life with his son in it and it didn't come easy. They would get to see each other every other weekend and that was far more than he had previously. That was the only way he could stomach it.

The next day, he still had to fight to see Joyce as Aubrey began to implement her scorched earth tactic. The judge ordered he meet Aubrey in the park with Joyce and let Charlie be "reintroduced" to his son over her supervision.

Aubrey and her lawyer fought this and tried to delay it to the next weekend, which Charlie's substitute attorney vehemently railed against as the two attorney built up the bill between each other. It was only after Charlie brought the fact the judge said directly, "tomorrow" to his substitute attorney, that his attorney argued that to Aubrey's attorney, who reviewed her notes and was forced to concede.

"This isn't going to be easy, Charlie," his substitute attorney said to him. "You're going to have to document every single occasion and incident. They are going to fight you tooth and nail." She was right. They fought Charlie on every single detail from the moment the temporary trial ended.

Sarah and Charlie got to spend a few more nights together before she had her return flight back to Hawaii. Her plan was to close up shop back in Kauai and formally give her job notice she was leaving and apply for a nursing job there in Wyoming. Sarah also wanted to let a little time pass before she joined Charlie in hope there would be resolution in some form between him and Aubrey.

"I want you to come back with me, Charlie," she said the night before her flight. "It doesn't matter what you do, they will hold it against you. If you fight this thing from afar, you won't get caught up in all the drama, Charlie. This place is your kryptonite and it always has been. Come back with me and let's live our life on our terms and not on the terms of some idiots from Sheridan who have never left that county."

Charlie thought about it and knew she was right, but also knew what he would lose if he didn't stand his ground and try to fight for his son. It was a difficult decision for him. There would be no easy answer and he knew this would be one of the most challenging times for him in his life.

He could easily jump on the plane and enjoy the good life back in Hawaii. It was the life he'd worked for and went there as if it were nothing on a Tuesday afternoon. He found love there again, just as he had in Moab. This time it was different, he told himself trying to convince his ego. This time he really did want to stay with Sarah for the rest of his life. That's how he felt now, he was certain of that.

"Come to think of it, that's how I felt about Mary and that's exactly how I felt about Aubrey," he told himself. "Maybe love is something we feel for the moment and it quickly fades away only to be replaced by something else. But this time it is different. Sarah is different and I'm different now. I love Sarah more than anyone I've loved in my life and more than myself."

He was torn. Deep down, he knew the only choice for him

to make had already been made. He had to stay and fight for his son, or he couldn't live with himself for the rest of his life. If he didn't fight and got on the plane to enjoy life and be happy, he knew it would destroy him in some form or fashion down the road. If he stayed, it would slowly destroy him in other ways.

"Sarah, you know I would love to catch that flight with you," he said to her after contemplating what he should do. "But you also know that I wouldn't be able to forgive myself if I didn't fight for Joyce now."

"I know, Charlie and you're a damn fool for it," she said to him, accepting his decision. "I'm going to be all alone on the island. It's going to be hard for both of us and I don't want to go into this telling each other how much we miss one another. I won't do that sort of thing. I find it disgusting really."

"I won't tell you how much I miss you, Sarah, but I'm going to miss you more than anything and I'm sorry I have to do this," he said.

"I forgive you and always will forgive you, Charlie," she said to him. "Just don't forget there's a bigger picture than this little fight and don't lose yourself in it."

The next morning, Charlie walked Sarah to her gate and they kissed and cried and made promises to each other. It made some of the other passengers uncomfortable, but they didn't care. Charlie watched as she walked out onto the tarmac and knew he should be getting on that plane with her.

"You idiot, Charlie," he said to himself. "You just let the girl of your dreams walk away on a flight to Hawaii and she wanted you to come with her to live forever. Instead, you chose to live in windy Wyoming and fight with your ex over a custody arrangement."

Sarah felt torn as she boarded the flight and looked out at Charlie driving off into the sunless morning.

Over the next week, Charlie got a job contracting with the National Park Service to pick native seeds at Devils Tower. He found the job online while scouring for anything to make a few bucks and was pleased when a doctor from Boulder, Colorado responded to his application. The doctor was an eccentric woman by Charlie's apprehension, but she was thorough and asked him so many questions it made him dizzy.

Her name was Doctor Leslie Burks. She was renowned for her ability to get projects done by the park service and they valued her efforts and paid her modestly for her work. They chose her for the Devils Tower project because they knew they could pay her the least of any of the contractors and she would get the job done no matter what. They had total faith they could underpay her and over receive. That was precisely the kind of deal they had in mind when they created the reseeding project.

It was a project to make the locals feel better about invasive species that were taking over the area. There was no stopping them now, but the Park Service wanted to create the impression they were doing something to mitigate the impact. The idea was to get a collection of native flora to the area and reseed it near the visitor center where the invasive species had taken ahold and were never going to be driven out now. The invasive species were all the weeds Charlie was familiar with growing up and the flowers they were collecting seeds for, he was also familiar with.

To him, it sounded like an adventure coupled with a good opportunity to collect his thoughts and gather himself all while getting to spend time in the same place Richard Dreyfuss had made famous with his performance in "Close Encounter of the Third Kind." Charlie heard about the movie all his life having been born in 1984, but he never really watched the 1977 film until 2016 when he watched it on a rainy afternoon while it was playing on television.

"That and Brokeback Mountain are what this state is famous for," he told Sarah on the phone. "Oh, and Matthew Shepard."

"Who was Matthew Shepard?" she asked Charlie.

"You've never heard of Matthew Shepard," he asked her in disbelief.

"No, I've never heard of him," she responded. "Who is he, now I'm curious."

Charlie went on to explain in detail the events that lead to Shepard's death in 1998 and how rescuers found him tied to a snow fence. Sarah had no conception of what a snow fence was, being from Louisiana and all, never having seen one in her life. Even after Charlie told her the history, she still had no recollection from her childhood of the event that affected so many in the country.

"One of the guys who did it was from Sheridan," Charlie said to her. "I met a guy who used to be a guard at the federal prison. He told me the guy still claims he had nothing to do with it and was just there. That he took the fall for the other guy who did most of the dirty work. Who knows what happened."

"The only people who know what happened there are them and their god," Sarah said to Charlie, sitting on a beach in Kekaha, Hawaii watching the sun go down in a blaze of glory over the ocean. "Charlie, I wish you were here."

"You know I wish I was, but the island never loved me as much as you, Sarah," he said. "She just wanted me to see paradise long enough to know I could never afford to live there. It's been amazing and unforgettable to be able to spend time with Joyce and to see him again. All that has been so good, but I do miss you and the island every day, Sarah. I can't wait to start our life together again and get through all this mess."

Sarah was intently looking forward to that day but dreaded the thought of leaving one of the best places in the world for Wyoming. To her, and everyone she talked to about the prospect, the mere thought was crazy.

She continued and made arrangements to move back to the mainland and did so with trepidation and fear about the move. Inside of her heart, she knew it was the right thing to do. She wanted to be there for Charlie through all of it and she wanted to build their life together and go forward.

Charlie and Dr. Burks, along with a few other hands, went about their days picking the native seeds of the Black Hills region. The mornings were spent meandering prairie dog towns, always looking for rattlesnakes with each step. When the afternoon sun began to shine, Charlie would catch himself marveling at the grandeur of that sacred column that is Devils Tower. The tower itself held greater meaning to Charlie now than it had ever in his life.

He'd visited it when he was younger with his grandfather who passed away several years ago now.

He took Charlie there when he was sick with cancer and knew the end was near. He wanted his grandkid to see the place where he had spent time when he was young.

"They say a girl was out here picking flowers for her mother long ago," Charlie's grandfather told him then. "She was spotted by the biggest bear on earth and he came tumbling down at her, roaring and ravaging the earth. The girl fell on her knees and began to pray and the more she prayed, the more the earth began to rise around her. The girl opened her eyes and saw the ground had risen into a giant column around where she fell on her knees and began to pray.

"The bear was furious and began to attempt to climb the column, but kept falling back down to the earth. He clawed and scratched as much as he could, but couldn't reach the girl who was now safe from the bear atop Devils Tower. The claw marks you can still see today." he said to Charlie, pointing to the perfectly symmetrical lines going up and down the rock that rises from the earth.

Charlie hadn't been back to Devils Tower since that time with his grandfather and now relished those times. Now, he had a different understanding of the place. He'd studied the Black Hills since first coming there and now knew Devils Tower was a sacred place to many tribes.

The Sioux held Devils Tower as the birthplace of wisdom and it was where they received the sacred White Buffalo Calf Pipe from White Buffalo Calf Woman who appeared to the Sioux when they were struggling and advised them to live in harmony with the world around them. The Sioux called the great rock column that rises out of a sea of prairie, Bearlodge, and many other names. The Sioux still hold sacred ceremonies there to this day.

In the Treaty of Fort Laramie of 1868, the government of the United States agreed to give ownership of the Black Hills to the Sioux, along with abandoning forts along the Bozeman Trail. When gold was discovered in the Black Hills soon thereafter and settlers moved along the Bozeman Trail at their leisure, oftentimes getting ransacked by marauding natives hell-bent on keeping the whites off of their sacred hunting grounds only they were supposed to be hunting on. The failures of the treaty led straight to an all-out war, culminating with the history-defining Custer's Last Stand. Charlie was surprised to learn the Sioux had sued the government for reparations in 1980 and as of the day he stood at Devils Tower, the interest on the reparations stood at over a billion American dollars, the measure of progress.

The Sioux refused the monetary compensation from the United States government failing on their terms of the treaty and many thereafter. The Sioux simply want their land back that was stolen from them under false pretenses.

Charlie found a knife casing decorated in beautiful beads while seed hunting one morning. The knife case was left on a deer carcass that had turned to bones over the long winter and hot summer sun.

"Leave it there," Burks told Charlie after seeing it, who was contemplating picking it up. "They leave it there as part of the hunting ritual. It may be new and it may be really old. I'll tell the park rangers where we found it and take a picture of it for them."

More and more Charlie started to feel the great power the first national monument held as he spent time there. He was grateful he'd received the opportunity to transition back to the mainland from Hawaii in a place like Devils Tower, however, he felt as though he and the culture that existed at that time were directly responsible for the stealing of these sacred places.

"We don't belong here doctor," he said one morning. "If anything, the native deserves to be here undisturbed. All I see here is a bunch of tourists who drive up to the monument where they built a road for them right to the base of the sacred column."

"The natives don't want them climbing on the rock either," Doctor Burks told him. "If it were up to them, not a single person without native blood would be allowed here. They just want their land back and this government would rather give them blankets with scarlet fever instead. It's going to be a long time before things are made right, Charlie. We have a small part to play in that right now, picking native seeds. It's a small start fixing a large problem. The more of the native element we can restore, the better off this place will be."

"It's hard to envision a world where we haven't stolen all the things anymore," Charlie said to her. "Every place I end up going to, it's the same story all over again. We as a country have taken everything we ever wanted with impunity. One day we are going to have to restore all the things we took by force back to the rightful owners or it will end up ending us as we have ended so many others."

With that, they continued picking the native seeds for another day, as that day and the weeks moved on and the project came to an end, Charlie knew he had learned something along the way. He'd gained a new respect for the land and he now saw it differently than he had ever witnessed it before. He wondered out loud if there would ever be a day it was given back to the Sioux along with the Black Hills. He also wondered if it somehow tied in with his plight of having things taken from him. If the people of the past could see the present and how a child could be taken from a father, causing him to fight for the basic right to see his child, would they be surprised?

"Is this just the perpetuation of stealing everything from everyone," Charlie asked himself while picking echinacea on the side of a hill. "They stole the kingdom of Hawaii from the Hawaiians and they still are trying to steal things like election victories from the Navajo. There's nothing sacred left in the world today and it is all for sale. It comes down to how much money and greed a person has."

Charlie wished this wasn't the truth or that wasn't how things were in the world, but he had seen it all firsthand now and there was no denying the entire world he knew, and the parts he never had a chance to know, were quickly getting a road built straight through them on the way to easier convenience and ease of access for the masses. There was no privacy in this new world of mechanized tourism. It didn't matter how many tons of garbage got created on the way to those places or how many billions of gallons of gas were being burned on the way. Just as long as they paid their entrance fees once they got to the park and left only their memories and footprints while taking as many photos as humanly possible mattered now.

Charlie was one of them and he knew it. He was a born tourist and always would be. None of these fantastic places would ever be his to experience as a place to call home. He would just merely pass through on the way to his next great adventure.

There was a time for him when it was special and he held claim to have a superior idea, but now as the realities of custody battles and politics set in their usual course of motion for a young man, Charlie found everything was rigged against him. No individualism could save the day or grant him an extra day in paradise, the world always beat a man down and forced him down that long and lonesome path back home, wherever that may be. The problem now was there wasn't a home to return to for Charlie. It had all been gobbled up by millionaires from the cities who had decades to get ahead and left little but scraps to be cleaned off the floor.

He was 32 and had no prospect of buying a home. Charlie's credit had been destroyed long ago by his attempt to better himself going to college. To do that, he unknowingly mortgaged his future by taking loans he could never repay.

Here he was, coming home to his son and he couldn't see him. As the job came to a close and Charlie packed up his gear, he said goodbye to the good doctor.

"Charlie, it was a pleasure to get to know you," Burks said to him as they finished loading up her car. "I have a long drive back to Boulder, but I just wanted to thank you for helping this project and I wish you the best in dealing with this situation involving your son. You did the right thing coming back to him like you did. These things have a way of working themselves out. We were short-handed on this project and I was worried we weren't going to be able to do it and then you came along and helped us meet our quota."

"It was a good thing to be able to come here," he said to her. "Thanks for giving me a chance to work on the project. I'm glad that something good might come out of all of this. If nothing else, it was a good way to get to see every view of that tower."

With that, the team said their final goodbyes, and Charlie drove back towards Sheridan with an uncertain future. On his way out of the campground, he rolled a cigarette exhaustively and was about to light it when he noticed a park ranger in the middle of the road stopping him.

His hand raised, he looked intently at Charlie through the windshield. The car Charlie was driving he had just purchased for $600 from a tattoo artist who needed to sell it before he moved to Michigan to pursue his dream of being a rapper.

"You don't have a license plate on your vehicle, sir," the ranger said to Charlie.

"I just bought the vehicle and in Wyoming, you can drive the vehicle with the bill of sale and purchase title for 30 days," he said to the man, who eyed Charlie suspiciously.

"I would like to see both, sir," the ranger said as Charlie dived through his glovebox and produced the documents for his inspection. "You are supposed to have this document notarized."

"It was a Sunday when I purchased the vehicle and the guy I bought it from was moving out of the state, so there was no possible way to get a notary that afternoon," he said.

"What's that in your hand, sir," the ranger asked, looking at the rolled cigarette Charlie had prepared.

"It's a rolled cigarette, would you like one," Charlie asked.

"Are you high, sir?" he asked. "You do know that I can search your entire vehicle if I liked?"

"Feel free to rummage through this old car, you won't find a single thing. Also, I believe you need to have probable cause or my permission to search the vehicle, sir," Charlie informed the ranger. "That's kind of important, especially considering I've been camping here as a contract worker for the Park Service."

"Get out of my park," the ranger told him, stepping out of the way after handing Charlie back his documents.

As Charlie drove away, he looked at the ranger in his rear-view mirror. He'd just received that infamous Wyoming treatment he knew would follow him throughout the process of trying to live there. It was par for the course in the grand scheme of things. He felt as though the ranger's treatment towards him was just a parting gift the Park Service rendered to him as a thank you for helping them with their seeding project.

For a moment he lamented the loss of paradise. He was so far from that world now and this is where he was going to stay until there could be some kind of resolution. He wanted nothing more than to simply get to be a father to his son, but now he would go into that fight headed to a trial almost a year away. He knew there would be no empathy or compromises for him. The only empathy and compromise would have to come from him. Charlie headed down the interstate knowing the storm he was headed into.

A few days later, on the last day of September, Charlie got a job as the local supplier of linens to businesses. His trainer showed him the ropes, starting every morning at 4:30 a.m., digging through bags full of dirty towels and uniforms. It was a hard transition and day after day he plunged forward with the thought he was doing it all to be closer to his son.

He would see his boy once a week for a three-hour visitation with him staying with Charlie every other weekend. They caught up and spent time laughing and enjoying their reunion. It hurt Charlie every time he had to say goodbye to the boy and he would call Sarah to tell her about it.

"I get to drive around the town and other nearby towns, picking up mats and bags of dirty linen," he told her one night. "I drive a giant box truck and people scoff at me as they walk by. It was the best job I could find here."

There were other jobs Charlie was qualified for, but the local newspaper had a superiority complex when it came to their publication that hadn't won an award in years. The publisher especially condemned Charlie as he frequently talked to her about some of the articles he deemed as journalistic flops.

"It's not forever, Charlie," Sarah reminded him. "Soon I'm going to be there and everything will be different. Us being together will make a world of difference."

The first week in October, Sarah took a flight to Sheridan, paid for by the local hospital that wanted to hire her.

"I was going to fly here to see you anyway, so it's just lucky they want to hire me," she told him in the small airport terminal after making people nervous in the baggage claim area with their public displays of affection. "Show me this town and what I'm getting myself into."

After showing Sarah the town of Sheridan again, which took no longer than 20 minutes, Sarah sighed knowing all too well the road that lay ahead. They went back to the treehouse and made love to escape the reality of the small town they were to reside in.

"We can't stay here for longer than a year," she proclaimed to Charlie. "There's nothing here for us. We can try as hard as we want to make it the place, but it will never be what we need."

"I need to be closer to my son for the time being," Charlie responded. "You know I would rather be in Hawaii doing what I love with you, but this has to be done."

"It might take a whole lot longer than you think, Charlie," she said matter of factly. "If there's one true thing in all of this it's that you love your boy. I can't wait to meet him."

They picked Joyce up for his first weekend with Charlie in over a year after they had a few supervised visits by Aubrey. Charlie couldn't understand how they wanted the person who held them apart for so long now to preside over their time together. To him, that was something that didn't make sense and added insult to injury.

It was a special day for the father and son, something they had both thought about for so long now. The boy smiled as his dad pulled up in a golden truck, getting out and beckoning his three-year-old to jump into his open arms. To the boy, none of the other stuff mattered or existed for right now he was able to be with his dad.

Charlie loaded the boy up in the back seat and calmly said to him," Joyce, this is Sarah. She's a friend your dad met in Hawaii."

The boy was shy, not talking, looking out the window and away from the estranged adults that sat in the front. To the boy, it was an insult to his mother to say hi and he knew she would not like it if he did so.

For Charlie, it was an introduction that had to be made.

He'd been dating Sarah for over six months and thought that sufficient time enough for them to become acquainted. The two were the most important people in the world to him and he wanted nothing more than for them to get along, but he knew there was significant difficulty that lay ahead.

For Sarah, Joyce was the first child who responded to her like that. Children loved her and flocked to her as bees flocked to flowers. Her smile and angelic demeanor comforted them, but not Joyce. He would look at her when she was not looking to look her over. When Sarah looked at him, he would quickly look away. Sarah looked at Charlie and smiled. They had done what they set out to do from the beginning and here they were, thousands of miles from where they started, trying to do something right in their minds, a world away from where they were. Through 34 years on this earth, she relished being next to the one she loved and the son he loved so much. It had been so long since she felt the comfort and freedom that comes with the feeling of love through her lover.

She knew it would be difficult. That thought didn't bother her, only the thought of the pain that would accompany it did. She hated to know Charlie endured so much through being held from his son. She knew that it tore him up inside to be held from Joyce. Sarah hoped the ones that did this to them paid for what they did. She didn't know how, but she just wanted there to be some sort of justice in the fact.

Charlie drove them up to the mountains and Tongue River Canyon where a series of caves laid at the end of the trail. Snow flickered slowly the higher they went, melting as it touched the ground below the fall foliage that shined a brilliant and vibrant yellow in the dim sunlight. Joyce was still looking away.

"How was your day," Charlie asked him.

Joyce continued to play the silent game and finally laughed when his dad made a fart joke. From there he started to smile. They got out of the car after parking at the trailhead.

Sarah made sure they had water and everything they needed for the small hike. She loved a good hike and was struck immediately by the scenic beauty surrounding them in the jagged and enormous boulders forming the canyon. The colors were at their peak, at the time when they were just about to fall from the tree. She had never seen fall foliage like this before and had never seen snow so early in the year before.

Joyce had never been in the mountains when he was conscious enough to know he was in the mountains. He wondered if Spiderman was out there hiding somewhere in the cliffs. He scanned the horizon hoping to catch a glimpse of his favorite superhero. In his hand, he clasped a Lego Spiderman. He had a habit of holding onto things when he was nervous.

"This is just a light dusting, Sarah," he said to her. "Wait a month or so and you will see the real Wyoming snow. Once you experience it you'll wish you never had."

"I've seen it snow before, Charlie," she said laughing at him. "It can't be worse than what I've seen in Portland right?"

"I don't know, you're going to have to wait and see," he said.

Joyce asked his father if he could go on his shoulders. The enormity of the landscape made him feel small and being just a little guy, he wanted the security that comes with being on his father's shoulders. His legs also began to ache and he was tired but didn't want to tell his dad that.

The world looked different perched atop his father for Joyce. He looked around nervously, gazing at the river below the trail, hissing, and flowing. He wanted to throw a rock in it. Charlie was just glad to have the two people he loved most in the world at that moment together.

Sarah wanted a dog and to be together with Weston back in Hawaii. She loved Charlie and was happy. But a part of her wanted to be back in paradise and blamed him for taking that from her for an illegitimate child he had out of wedlock. She cursed god that she was so unlucky in her choice of men that she had to fall for a man with a child that lived in Wyoming of all places.

She loved him and was willing to take the good with the bad.

To her, October was still a very warm time of year. She was not prepared for the winter ahead that had made countless women leave Wyoming in the spring after their first winter.

Joyce got down and walked with them along the trail. He started to gain a little confidence in his ability to hop the trail and by the end of the hike was running ahead of Sarah and Charlie to see what was ahead of them.

"Are you happy?" Sarah asked Charlie.

He thought for a second and looked at his son and then at her.

"I'm as happy as I can be," he said, lying to himself. In truth, he wanted everything that he didn't have, but there was no way he could admit it. "I'm only happy if you're happy, Sarah."

The West and the world came into a plague

It became a familiar routine for Charlie, Sarah, and Joyce. Charlie lived down the street from his young son, but saw him every other weekend, with a weekday visitation on Wednesday for three hours. Charlie struggled to tell his son he couldn't see him when Joyce asked if his dad could pick him up when they talked on the phone. Charlie had to tell him he couldn't.

Charlie pleaded with Aubrey to let him see his son more, but to her it was easy revenge, wanting him to know a woman's scorn held no bounds. She looked at it as if Charlie had bailed out on the hard parts of raising the child and cursed him for trying to come back into the fold to enjoy the fruits of her labor. She resolved to make it as hard as possible on Charlie at every turn. At every step of the way, she knew the law sided with her. All she had to do is wait him out, she thought, thinking Charlie would tire of Wyoming and leave as he always had.

Most of all, she wanted him to come to her and ask for forgiveness and make things right. She wanted that more than any vengeance, wanting what was now lost. He only wanted to have a relationship free of her and with his son, but out of stubbornness and anger, they never truly attempted to do what was best for their child. Lawyers were more effective for doing what they didn't want to do themselves.

Charlie was more stubborn than Aubrey gave him credit for and he dug in, aided by the arrival of Sarah who said her difficult goodbye to the island.

"It's not forever," she told the island and her friends the night before she left Kauai, watching the moon rise over the ocean for the last time.

With that, she boarded a plane the next morning and made her way across the ocean towards her new home, which was colder than she could have possibly imagined. The moving had been a process for her and at times she felt as though she was making the biggest mistake of her life. A fresh winter in the west awaited her with a temperature of negative 17 degrees Fahrenheit.

The first few weeks were hard on Sarah. Charlie met her at the airport in Seattle and they drove through the Northwest. They romped through Idaho, Montana, and down into their destination of Wyoming. The heater in the truck they had shipped from Hawaii had been bypassed and they were without heat for most of the drive, aside from the small heater Charlie purchased in Tacoma, Washington.

"Damn that Joel Fryer," Charlie cursed in the blasting cold that seeped through the truck as they leaped down the highway toward the Intermountain West.

Charlie had Sarah wrap herself in a blanket with the small car heater blowing directly into a funnel through the blanket by her feet. She'd never felt that kind of numbing cold in her life as they took a "detour" near Helena, she swore her limbs were freezing. They both saw a woman driving in front of them hit a black bear. Charlie and Sarah were so focused on the cold, they didn't get out to help the woman tend to the bear she had hit. Charlie thought they wouldn't have been of much use out in the November cold considering the condition they were already in.

When they reached the Wyoming border, Sarah was eased by the Big Horn Mountains, marking her arrival as a resident of the least populated state in the union. She was ready to be where they were going and all the getting there was behind them. She looked forward to staying rather than going for once.

Charlie tried to warn her of the bitter cold and how it was to live there. He failed to describe the ideology presiding in their new home and truly thought she would understand better as time passed. He hoped she would find happiness there, but feared it was simply too narrow for her and the persistent limitations he felt there would be the same for her. He thought she would find herself feeling on an island of a different kind than the one she had just left. He knew all too well how most handled Wyoming, leaving after the first winter. Or there was the other side of the coin where they moved there and fell in love and never left, telling everyone how much they love the place. There was no in between the two categories of people who moved there. Mostly, there was the type who moved there with an idea of what it would be like, quickly finding out the reality of the situation before leaving. It was a tough place where the people and the landscape showed it.

To Charlie, Wyoming was a state of resistance. One of the last places in the United States where you could smoke a cigarette inside while drinking a beer. That to him was something to be proud of in itself because the rest of the world had gone soft. He felt a kind of warmth in the resistance to the passing of time there. It was something he tried to do himself, but could never do it as well.

Charlie, like Sarah, also knew how hard it was to leave the island. The longing you felt for the ocean and the birds greeting the morning from paradise. It was hard to readjust to life on the mainland. He knew it would bring Sarah closer to a mundane reality that existed in the cold gray winter of the place.

Charlie tried like a typical transplant to make it more like home for her, buying flowers and pouring on the optimism in abundance. The first winter storm hit only a few days after Sarah arrived. It came in with ice driven winds that blew a thick layer of sleet with it, turning everything to a tundra that was normally later in the winter but had arrived earlier that year. The temperature dropped to below zero with the sun now absent until well into the morning and set just after four in the afternoon.

Sarah sat and looked at the arctic blast that blew in mercilessly out the safety of the front window. She grew depressed at her current lot in life and began to cry.

"It's ok, this is just how it is in the winter," Charlie said to her. "You'll get used to it after a little while."

She stared out into the cold and feared going into it. It made her cold just to look at it, let alone think about having to get used to it.

"You took me to the Russia of the United States," she said to him crying harder now. He came to her, trying to comfort her.

"It's just a little frozen water, there's nothing to be scared of," he said to her. Deep down he knew that it was a frozen barren wasteland and that he had taken her from one of the best places in the world to a place the outside world considered nearly non-existent or something you fly over unless you're visiting Yellowstone.

"If you ask someone if they have been to Wyoming, they will tell you that they have been to Jackson Hole or Yellowstone and that they love it," he said to Sarah. "But that's not what Wyoming is. Wyoming is a small town that's barren and windblown. It's winter eight months out of the year and then in the summers sometimes it never really gets warm."

That morning, Sarah got her first taste of driving in winter conditions. The sliding and ice on the roads scared her to the point of not wanting to drive. She drove as slowly as she possibly could, letting out a scream every time she felt the wheels start to slip. To make matters worse, the truck they had brought from the island didn't have functioning heat as they found out on the ride through Montana, so Charlie had her drive the small cheap car he had purchased for $600.

Charlie named the car "Blanca" even though the dirt and grime from the snow and salt on the roads made it a dirt white. Sarah drove that little car up the hill to the hospital she worked at. They were shocked she made it through her first week there the way she was crying hysterically when she made it to work through the first storm.

When she made it to work that first morning, she gained a little respect from the other nurses who were taking bets on how long she would last there. She also gained respect for them.

"Just take it one day at a time," she told herself while crying. "You've been in tough situations before. If the snow and the cold are the hardest things you have to get through here, then you will be just fine. It's all for the person I love and that's what keeps me going."

As the days went on and the nights got longer and the sunshine shorter, they both found themselves suffering from a lack of vitamin D. It was something that crept on in the winter months and gradually wore you down until you found yourself in the middle of winter with little to no sunshine as your soul starts to feel as if it will freeze all the way through.

There had never been a lack of sunshine in the life of Sarah Francois or a lack of the prospect of sunshine. Her life had been one of unconditional love and learning dotted with unlucky business with men.

Because of her past luck with men and the coldness of the world there, Sarah began to question what she was doing and if she hadn't made the biggest mistake of her life again. She was beginning to understand why the aunties would tell her, "I'm so sorry," when she told them she was moving to Wyoming when she was leaving in Kauai. She didn't understand the way of life in Wyoming and why people mirrored the environment they lived in there. Most of the people who lived there were born and raised there. Most of them had never really gotten the opportunity to travel outside of that small pocket of the world and they formed their opinion of the world from that experience. People like Charlie and Sarah were alien to them and they could never understand why anyone in their right mind would live in so many different places or move so often.

"They just stare at me here, Charlie," she said to him one night. "Why do they just stare at people like that? It makes me feel uneasy when they do that and they all do that to me like I'm a doll out of place in the dollhouse."

"They do it because you're something different to look at for them," he said to her. "They never get to see someone with real aloha. They know everyone in this town and it throws them off to see a different person than they're used to. Their central processing units have trouble computing it, so they stare. It's nothing to worry about, I like to stare back at them when they do it. When I first came here it was weird to me, but after a while you sort of get used to it. It's one of the things that make this place what it is, good ol' fashioned judgement."

"It makes me feel uncomfortable," she said.
Charlie tried to show her all the local watering holes, some of

them were famous in that small town. The Mint Bar was a draw
at one time in Sheridan with the famous line 'check you guns in at
the bar,' but it had seen better days and finally banned smoking
indoors after it had been done for over a hundred years there.

There was another nearby bar named The Rainbow where
the patrons and owner smoked inside despite the statewide ban on
indoor smoking. All of these places Charlie had frequented when
Sarah was still in Hawaii as he tried to adjust to the change in circumstances. Now that she was there with him, he tried to introduce her to the people he had made acquaintances with while she
was gone. Even if Charlie had made acquaintances with bartenders
and bar owners, he was not friends with any of these people like
the way he was friends with Joel, or The Sir.

"I can't make friends here, Charlie," Sarah would tell him.
"I just don't have anything in common with these people. They're
different people than I am. Someone told me everything was going
to be fine because Donald Trump isn't going to let the liberals take
over the country."

"That's the way they are here, Sarah," he said after laughing. "These are just simple country folk like where you're from.
They believe he is going to save coal and look out for them."

"I can't understand how they think that when they're getting laid off," she said. "He just keeps lying to them and robbing
them blind and they keep listening to what he says. I really have
no idea how they can follow the man. It's baffling to me. And
honestly, I really don't want to live in a place where they follow
everything a man like that says as if it's some kind of gospel. It's
the same back home, but more people question it there than here I
think. I don't know, maybe I'm wrong about that."

Charlie hated his job and longed to be back on the island
writing news articles about the county council, or dealing with
the mayor's people on account of not being allowed to talk directly
with the mayor himself. He missed chasing away the fiends in the
fields and the white owls.

He watched everything happening on the garden island intently with a focus on what he would do if he were there. His time
on Kauai to him now was like a dream in the tropical night. Like a

distant memory in the not so distant past.

He loathed all those who forced him out of his paradise to come back to the closed-minded ideology that plagued Wyoming. Most of all himself.

"This place is 30 years behind," he told Sarah. "I wish there were things I could do to change the way it is here. That's what all the transplants try to do here. They try to make this place like home. That's kind of what everyone does everywhere, it's not unique in that way. But nature here is something not many places can rival. It has things that make you want to stay forever, but things that make you want to never come back. Those are the redeeming qualities. There's a beauty in the simplicity."

Charlie had a sorted past with the place, having lived there some 20 years earlier. His mom moved there when he was young and he used to come and stay with her in Sheridan in the summers and holidays.

"Just try to spread the aloha here, Charlie," Sarah said to him. "They might be unhappy when it comes down to it and they don't know any different. If you show them the slightest aloha, maybe they'll respond."

"I've tried that here while you were gone, these people are immune to that type of stuff," he said to her. She heard him but didn't believe he was open enough to any other truth. "There's just too thick a love for the Republican Party and Donald Trump for them to believe anything different. The only thing that exists here is the winter. That's the only constant. That and jobs like the one I'm doing now."

They were silent for a minute on exactly what Charlie was doing now, which was collecting mats at the entrances of nearly all the buildings in Sheridan and Buffalo. He drove around to the government buildings and local businesses that had invested in a five-year contract they couldn't opt-out of without paying a steep fine for the mats to be changed weekly, bi-weekly, or monthly. The businesses and government were charged at an exploding high rate they could never get out of. They were legally obligated to put mats at entrances because the snow and moisture accumulation. People often fell in the snow and ice outside of buildings, accounting for a majority of emergency room visits in the town.

In addition to the mats, Charlie did all the linens, towels, and uniforms for many of the local companies. He got a commission on the route and it was just enough for him to pay the lawyers and be able to take Joyce and Sarah to places they had never been around the state.

For Charlie, the job was a meaningless racket he'd stumbled on. He needed it to look like he was trying to play the game to the powers that be. It was a job they wanted him to stay with for the rest of his life and pay his monthly dues with.

It was the Wyoming and conservative grand idea of what a father was, someone who didn't want to have all the responsibility but got enough time to go hunting with the boy when the fall came around. They wanted the boy to be able to visit his father rather than actively live with the father because no father replaced a mother. This was their stance and at the time there were only a handful of men in the state who had custody of their children. It perpetuated the problems of the place and the problem itself was nearly impossible for them to see.

Aubrey and her family made fun of Charlie, moving back to the small little town to turn mats and drive a white box truck. Charlie had to swallow more than his ego as he cleaned the dirty rags and linens of the restaurants and businesses in town. Many of the laundy marinated for a week before Charlie picked it up, often times making him gag and nearly throw up.

Thoughts of his son kept him going and working toward a goal, working towards doing just one thing right this time around. Charlie knew the time with Joyce at his age was important in so many ways for his development, but he felt trapped in the hate and litigation. He knew Aubrey and her family wanted him gone — to leave and never come back. Attempts to find a solution were always turned down on both sides as the winter perpetuated cold and stillness.

It wasn't only Aubrey who wanted Charlie to leave Sheridan for good and never come back. Sarah wanted to make a living in a different place where they would be free of Charlie's illegitimate son and prior obligations. She didn't dare tell him that's how she felt about Joyce unless she had too much to drink and they were at odds with each other. Then she would tell him with full force just exactly how she felt about the situation.

"There's nothing here for us, Charlie," she railed at him one night. "The only thing here is our end. This place will drive you crazy if you keep drinking and fighting like this. You'll lose your mind with all the lawyers and the shit. There's absolutely nothing here for you but a heart attack."

"That's not true," he said. "There's something here for us. Maybe it's not what we wanted or thought we'd have right now, but there's a reason we're here, Sarah. I have to be here for him right now. That doesn't mean forever, it means I have to see this thing through. It's the only way through it right now for me."

"I don't want to stay here longer than two years," she told him. "There's no way I could keep my sanity after that. The hospital here is nice. It's brand new and has some of the best equipment, but it's the people and their system that make it impossible. It's like there's a box they need to be in to function. They really can't think outside the box or for themselves from what I've seen. I don't know if it's a regional thing, but I haven't met anyone who seemed like I could be their friend. Maybe it's just me?"

They were at odds more often as the winter progressed. Fighting over little things and not smiling as much as they used to. They went to Yellowstone in the dead of the winter, just after Valentine's Day. It was a retreat for the two of them away from the small town that was starting to consume them both. They saw wolves and elk, and herds of bison congregating in an attempt to escape the winter cold.

The custody trial loomed in May and they tried to do what they could to remain happy, but it was hard for them as the ides of March rolled in and they yearned for the warmth of spring. They both fell ill in late February. Sarah came down with what was diagnosed as pneumonia, spreading it to Charlie. Charlie didn't believe it could spread to him if it was pneumonia and exactly five days after Sarah fell sick, he fell deathly ill.

They both laid out for some time from the pneumonia-like sickness, Sarah recovering first and then Charlie. They both lost their sense of smell and taste.

The spring refused to come in Wyoming as the cold never subsided and they watched the early days of the Coronavirus spread through the nation. At first, the people in Sheridan would joke about how they better watch out or they would get the "rona." That was in late February.

Charlie would listen as he sat in the steam room as baby boomers talked about the virus like there was no way it could come to Wyoming. It was the nature of the people in Wyoming to think they were quarantined from the rest of the world anyway and that what happened in Wyoming was completely different from what was happening in the populated centers of the country. The rural areas, and especially the Intermountain West saw few cases at first.

But then the closures started happening and terms like "social distancing," and "stay six feet apart," and "wear a mask," became the new normal as restaurants and bars shut down, along with hair salons. Stay at home orders were issued in several states. Wyoming never went as far as to order stay at home orders, but they closed national and state parks. People there resisted masks and banded together with states like South Dakota and their governor Kristi Noem who tried to oppose shutdowns. Wyoming wanted to leave the safety of the citizens up to themselves and there were jokes from local politicians in Jackson that you can't "cowboy up" in a global pandemic.

By March 11, the first case of the virus appeared in Sheridan. Soon there were three cases and the businesses Charlie serviced began to close their front doors one by one. Sarah was working while Charlie watched president Trump speak about the virus on March 15. Charlie was drunk but thought president Trump sounded drunker than he was the way he was talking about the virus.

"You don't have to buy so much, take it easy, just relax," Trump said during one of his daily press conferences on March 15. "People are going in and are buying more. I remember I guess during the conversation, Doug of Walmart said, 'they buy more than they buy at Christmas.' Relax, we're doing great. It all will pass."

But it didn't pass and there was a national toilet paper crisis as people began dying in mass from the virus and store shelves suddenly turned bare as panic shopping took over with many believing it was the end of times, and the plague was just one of the ways god was punishing the wickedness of the United States.

President Trump halted his daily press conferences after comments were made and interpreted about injecting disinfectant intravenously as a possible cure. The rules changed daily on local levels. Some places would rescind mask mandates after public pressure and protests demanded mask mandates be lifted. Eventually, even in Wyoming, the masks became a constant.

Infection levels began to skyrocket in Louisiana and New York, then jumping to other areas. By April, the virus had not made significant progress in Wyoming, but had devistated many densly poplutated cities.

Many in Wyoming wanted to open up earlier than they did when the governor lifted closures in May. Many businesses never closed, in fact, many did well during the first shutdown. And many didn't do so well.

Joyce asked Charlie why George Floyd was killed in late May and June. Charlie never had a good answer why.

The businesses told Charlie about their struggles, but he couldn't believe they just kept paying for unnecessary services such as mat service during a depression. It was a system, he thought. A system that couldn't withstand a virus that requires attention and a cohesive effort. He wondered to himself if it was all going to collapse.

Sarah and Charlie continued to take Joyce to places like Mount Rushmore, Devils Tower, Yellowstone, the Grand Tetons, and the hot springs town of Thermopolis. There was never enough time it seemed.

It snowed on Easter Sunday that year, making Sarah cry. She couldn't help it, the snow made her heart sad. Nobody in her family could believe such a thing as living somewhere where it could snow on Easter Sunday.

Not only did it snow, but it was a blizzard.

"It just happens in the west," he tried to explain to her. "It's just the way it is. Sometimes it gets the trees just when they leaf out and destroys them. The trees have to start all over again."

Sarah tried to hide her anxiety and frustration with the Wyoming situation. She was beginning to think she couldn't hold on anymore. There was no reason, she thought, to keep herself locked in a cage in the most conservative place in the union. She was beginning to hate coming home from work and seeing Charlie drunk in his depression and obsession with the custody battle which had just been postponed due to the pandemic.

"Charlie, you can't hold on to this battle," she said to him in hopes of persuading him to see the writing on the wall. "This will drive you insane like I've told you all along. At some point, you're going to have to accept this isn't going to turn out how you envisioned."

"I don't know how I envisioned it," he answered. "There was no end goal, just a hope they would let me see my son and be his dad. They're going to make me fight for that."

After a two month delay, Charlie got his day in court. Wyoming and most of the country had opened everything back by the time of the trial, which was in the middle of July. By that time, over 135,000 people had died of the virus in the country. Wyoming accounted for 21 of those deaths and many held a certain pride in that number at that time. Many Wyomingites believed the virus was completely made up and a tool of the democrats to win the election because Donald J. Trump was doing so well at destroying the liberal agenda.

Charlie tried to play it neutral and just get through the trial without being arrested or apprehended for having loyalties to anyone other than Donald Trump.

"I'm going to take this matter under advisement," the judge said after the six hour trial for custody of young Joyce.

Outside the courthouse, Charlie's lawyer told him the judge could take anywhere from one day to three weeks to decide on the case. He told him to just hold tight and wait until there was an order.

Eight weeks later, after the summer, Charlie was informed

of the judge's decree.

They took away any decision making ability from Charlie, granting Aubrey the same schedule they had done for over a year. Charlie Porter left paradise to get the right to be with his son every other weekend. The judge did give him more time with Joyce in the summer and on the holidays.

Joyce grew more comfortable with his dad and with Sarah as the year progressed. Sarah in time grew to love the wilderness that existed in Wyoming, cherishing the high mountain lakes and wildlife they got to see together. They got a dog and took him camping with them the first day they picked him up and separated him from his mother and the rest of the litter.

In November, Donald Trump lost the presidency to Joe Biden, bringing an end to the Trump era.

Near Christmas, when the plague was at a peak in Wyoming that fateful year of 2020, Charlie asked Sarah to marry him after she was giving him a hard time for smoking cigarettes in front of Joyce.

"We've seen paradise, and we've seen the plague," he said to her on one knee. "But all I know is I want to be in both with you. Wherever we are, we're always going to be together."

She said yes, even though she should have probably known better.

"Was all the suffering worth it?" he asked her.

"You haven't suffered yet," she said to him.

The End

Ryan Mitchel Collins

Ryan Mitchel Collins was born in the high sagebrush plain town of Craig, Colorado in 1986. He studied creative writing at Colorado State University before publishing 'Everyone Dies Alone' in 2013 and 'For the Sake of Tomorrow' in 2016. Collins has served as a newspaper editor/journalist in Utah, Wyoming, North Dakota, Colorado, and Hawaii. He looks forward to teaching his son to catch big fish and to be a decent human.

Powder River Publishing is located in Buffalo Wyoming, specializing in contemporary literary fiction and contemporary Western fiction.

www.powderriverpublishing.com